"What about the polo game?" Dusty called.

She'd seen the light. Surely. She had to come to her senses in every area. Right? "It's over. Off the table. We'll have a normal rodeo now."

Max shook her head slowly, and a fierce determination carved her stubborn jaw hard.

"The polo stays."

"But—"

"It's weird and it will draw a crowd. Mark my words." She pointed to him. "You get the bull riding." She jabbed her own chest with her thumb. "I get the polo match."

She turned away to enter the outbuilding, but tossed back over her shoulder, "Do your job, Dustin. Convince those people to come for the bulls and to stay for the ponies."

The slamming of the door echoed across the yard.

Dusty clenched his fists to stop himself from punching a hole in the wall of the house. Lordy!

Max could drive a man to drink.

Dear Reader,

This is the sixth and last book in my Rodeo, Montana series. When I finish a series, it truly feels like I'm leaving old friends and it's sad to say goodbye.

I'm glad I was able to give each of the women of the Rodeo Fair Revival Committee her own happy ending.

Max intrigued me right from the start. She's grouchy and argumentative and vulnerable. It made sense to me to give her a happy-go-lucky, carefree, handsome rodeo star.

Dusty has charmed every woman he's ever met, but he can't charm Max. No way, no how. She's immune.

When his mother tells him that he's finally met his match, Dusty balks. Of course, these opposites attract so much that nothing can keep them apart in the end.

I hope you have enjoyed reading my Rodeo series as much as I have enjoyed writing every single book.

Thank you for joining me on my journey,

Mary Sullivan

HOME *on the* RANCH
MONTANA RODEO STAR

—— ✦ ——

MARY SULLIVAN

H **HARLEQUIN**® HOME ON THE RANCH

Recycling programs
for this product may
not exist in your area.

ISBN-13: 978-1-335-50867-6

Home on the Ranch: Montana Rodeo Star

Printed in U.S.A.

™ www.Harlequin.com

Award-winning author **Mary Sullivan** realized her love for romance novels when her mother insisted she read one. After years of creative pursuits, she discovered she was destined to write heartfelt stories of love, family and happily-ever-after.

Her first book, *No Ordinary Cowboy*, was a finalist for the Romance Writers of America's prestigious Golden Heart® Award in 2005. Since then, Mary has garnered awards, accolades and glowing reviews.

Mary indulges her passion for puzzles, cooking and meeting new people in her hometown of Toronto. Follow her on Facebook, Facebook.com/marysullivanauthor, to learn more about her and the small towns she creates.

MarySullivanBooks.com

Books by Mary Sullivan

Harlequin Western Romance

Rodeo, Montana

Rodeo Father
Rodeo Rancher
Rodeo Baby
Rodeo Sheriff
Rodeo Family

Harlequin Superromance

Cody's Come Home
Safe in Noah's Arms
No Ordinary Home

Visit the Author Profile page
at Harlequin.com for more titles.

I would like to dedicate this book to every writer, published and unpublished, who has ever supported my writing. I've traveled with amazing people throughout this fabulous journey. You have enriched my life. I wish you all the best with your own writing careers.

Chapter 1

Life was good.

The tires of Dustin Lincoln's pickup hummed a getting-there tune on the small highway that led to Rodeo, Montana. Through the open windows, wind ruffled his hair at ninety miles an hour, above the speed limit, sure, but not by much. No sense being foolish and overdoing it so close to his destination.

His thumb beat the steering wheel in time to Blake Shelton's "Doing It to Country Songs" blaring from the radio.

On Saturday night, he'd had a fine time accomplishing exactly that with a pretty blonde buckle bunny in Colorado after his rodeo win.

Any minute now, he'd reach his temporary home and job for the next month. All it would require of him was a little subterfuge on his part, hardly worth a mention, and just the barest use of any acting skills he could dredge up.

With a little luck, while he was at it, he would also win the bull-riding competition in the rodeo that would end the two-week fair and bring home big bucks.

"Luck, Dusty? Who're you kidding? You got talent," he bragged to the empty cab. "Raw talent. It's what brings home the bacon every time. Right, Thunder?"

He glanced in his mirrors, catching sight of the horse trailer being towed behind him, carrying his trusty Appaloosa.

And now he was talking to his horse.

With the past weekend's pot along with his salary for the next month, and if he could win the bull-riding event at Rodeo's fair, plus any other wins he could garner through the fall, he'd have a sizable nest egg to get him through the winter with leftover money for his retirement account.

Sweat formed at the thought of retirement, so Dusty did what he always did—pushed it out of his mind and whistled to the next song on the radio.

He had another ten years of rodeo-event participation in him. At least.

At thirty-one, he wasn't anywhere close to throwing in the towel.

No *way* could he lose the Rodeo Fair bull-riding event. He was on a roll.

All he had to do first was convince some imprudent woman to cancel some other dumb competition she'd planned. Some nontraditional event she was trying to slip into the town's rodeo. Or so he'd heard from his dad.

His presence in Rodeo was strictly as a favor for Dad's longtime buddy Marvin. So what if that woman had no idea he wasn't really working for her? He'd head to her ranch and work with her for the next month to plan a rodeo that contained no surprises, as agreed. And when the job was done, he'd be on the road again. No harm done, really. It would all work out in the end.

That didn't mean Dusty couldn't enjoy himself, enter the rodeo and win some money while he was here.

Not to mention yet another rodeo buckle.

He laughed for the pure pleasure of driving down a sun-lit highway on a carefree day.

He'd been on the road for a good three hours already. His left knee protested.

Nope. Not allowed. His knee was fine. Absolutely okey-dokey.

If when he adjusted his position it pained him a bit, that was only because the drive had been long.

Purely stiffness. Just normal stuff.

Before reaching town, he slowed to sixty, a mere crawl, his attention caught by an amusement park with a brightly colored carousel in pride of place front and center.

Strangest merry-go-round ever.

Was that a…a *bull*? And a pair of bighorn sheep? And an elk and a white-tailed deer? All wore elaborately painted-on saddles.

Weirdest damned thing.

He glanced at the wrought iron sign arching over the entrance to the park.

Rodeo, Montana, Fairgrounds
and Amusement Park
Home of Our World-Famous Rodeo

Yeah! Rodeo was his game and bull riding his calling. Fitting that the carousel had a big old bull for kids to ride.

Start 'em early, he always said.

Now to locate this Max who'd hired him to help organize the rodeo and get this show on the *road*. In no time, he'd get her head turned around in the right direction where this cockamamy event was concerned.

Eager to get both his horse and himself settled in, he rode toward the town he could see on the horizon a half a mile or so along the highway, with the radio blaring another Blake Shelton song, "Straight Outta Cold Beer."

Now, *that* would be a crime.

The gas tank was full, his libido satisfied, his pockets flush and his belly about to be sated over lunch with his new boss.

"Yeeehaaawww!" Dusty Lincoln sure loved life.

Maxine Porter sat in a booth facing the front door of Violet Summer's Summertime Diner.

Vy stood beside the table, retro polka-dot dress flaring over generous hips and snug across an ample chest.

Max drummed her fingers on her thighs. "I don't have all day to wait for one slow man."

"Who?" Vy asked, setting down a cup of coffee in front of Max. "What man?"

"A guy named Dustin Lincoln. I hired him to help organize the rodeo. I'm running out of time."

Max sensed Vy stiffening. She'd known there would be resistance. That was why she hadn't said anything, but preferred to present the fair and rodeo revival committee with a fait accompli. They weren't about to un-hire someone once he was already in town.

"You *hired* someone?" Vy asked, voice low and ominous sounding. "This is the first I've heard of it. Is it in the budget? Did Samantha approve?"

The committee's accountant, Samantha Read, had been putting the kibosh on too many things, in Max's opinion. Fiscal responsibility was all well and good, but Max was overwhelmed and needed help.

"Well?" Vy pushed. Max loved the daylights out of her, but sometimes her persistence got on Max's nerves. "Did Samantha okay this expense?"

Max sipped her coffee, hot and black. "Nope. I made an executive decision, so to speak. Okay? We'll make enough profit out of the event."

Vy leaned her hip against the table. "And if we don't? Are you going to pay for his salary out of your own pocket?"

That was exactly Max's fear.

"Quit scowling at me, Vy." Max set her cup down onto the saucer so hard coffee sloshed. She grabbed a serviette to sop it up. "I'm doing what I have to do. I've got a ranch to run and chores to get to and bills to pay and a son to raise and a rodeo to plan and where the hell *is* this guy?"

She checked her watch again. Five minutes to noon and no sign of the new employee. If this was the way he planned to start, they were in for a rocky ride.

Vy stared at Max's hands. "For the love of all that's holy about responsible grooming, Max, you've got hangnails on top of hangnails."

Her hands? Max had just hired someone without the committee's permission and Vy was ready to give up and talk about Max's *hands*?

What was wrong with this picture?

Vy pulled a travel-sized tube of hand cream out of her apron pocket and tossed it onto the table. "Here. Use it."

Not a single torn cuticle marred Vy's perfectly manicured red nails.

Max applied a small dot of cream to her palm.

"More," Vy said.

Max squirted again and a splat of cream burst out of the tube. She pushed up her sleeves and rubbed cream over her hands, wrists and forearms.

"Fat lot of good this is going to do with all the chores I have to face when I get home."

"You can at least try to take care of yourse—" Vy broke off and stared out the window. "Wow. *Who* is *that*?"

The bell above the door tinkled. A man stepped in and stood for a moment, silhouetted against sunny Main Street behind him. Not just any man. A young god.

Max stared at six feet of blond male *perfection*. And judging by his dimpled grin, didn't he know how perfect he was?

The walls of the diner expanded with the combined sighs of the female inhabitants of the large room.

He entered the space as though he owned it.

Well-used cowboy boots, worn blue jeans faded across the fronts of his thighs and a denim shirt with rolled-up sleeves exposing strong forearms dusted with golden hair proclaimed that this was a real working cowboy. So did his trim, muscled body.

His jewelry, though, testified to ego in Max's opinion. What cowboy wore jade?

Apparently, this one did—on his wrist, locked in a big hunk of gnarly silver, and at his waist, decorating a belt buckle the size of the state of Montana.

The worst offense, in Max's opinion, was the choker around his neck…or whatever it would be called on a man.

It looked like crocheted rope or sisal, but neither of those would be comfortable. She wouldn't have thought the blue beads would be, either.

Dear Lord, no cowboy worth his salt wore macramé… and certainly not on his throat.

Vy approached him and said, "Take a seat wherever you want." By the breathy tone lacking her customary sarcasm, Vy had fallen under his spell.

Remember your husband? Max wanted to yell. *Remember Sam, the guy you love?*

The blond god laughed and gifted Vy with a swift appreciative once-over from deep blue eyes. Vy smiled in return, an acceptance of mutual attraction, the international language between men and women that Max had never mastered, like a secret handshake she didn't understand.

No one had ever given her the code.

A rueful twist of the guy's lips acknowledged Vy's newly burgeoning pregnant tummy. He shrugged as though to say, *In another time and another place we could have been friends.*

Friends with benefits, judging by his grin and the twinkle in his eyes.

He shifted on his feet and hooked a thumb into one pocket. "I'm meeting someone here. A woman named Max."

Vy turned and pointed at Maxine. Every pair of eyes in the diner followed the direction of her arm. "*That* is Max."

Max's cheeks heated. Why, oh, why, had she decided to make this meeting public? For good reason, she reminded herself. She hadn't wanted a stranger on her ranch until she met him and took his measure.

Like a mother bear, she protected her family, not to mention her privacy.

She stood.

The man's startled gaze did a quick slide down her body and back up to her face. His expression flattened, not at all the charming reaction he'd had to Vy.

She knew what he saw: a woman with not one trace of femininity.

Well, tough.

She was who she was.

He would accept her or he wouldn't get the job.

Period.

She held out her hand. "I'm Max Porter." One swift, hard handshake welcomed him to Rodeo with about as warm a reception as she had in her to offer.

"Dusty Lincoln," he said, voice deep. "Pleased to meet you." He stared at the hand Max had just shaken and wiped it on his pant leg.

Great. She'd just smeared skin cream on the guy.

He looked confused.

So was she.

She had expected a talented, smart rodeo rider to help her. She hadn't anticipated male beauty.

Damn. She hoped the female population wouldn't cause problems. The last thing the upcoming summer fair needed was to be sidetracked by events outside of the rodeo.

"Sit," she said and slid into the booth.

He slid in more slowly, wary, maybe because she hadn't fallen in a girlie heap at his perfect feet.

"Max?" he said, resting his hat on the seat beside him in the leather booth.

"Maxine," Vy clarified and Max scowled.

"Max works for me," she said, sounding ungracious, but, God, she was tired.

"What can I get for you, Dustin?" Vy asked.

"Everyone calls me Dusty." He shared a smile with Vy.

After a perusal of the menu sitting in front of him on the table, Dusty ordered meat loaf and garlic smashed potatoes.

They used to be mashed potatoes. Now they were smashed. Apparently, that meant you could leave in the lumps. No one else complained. Only Max. Everyone else was happy to jump on the latest trending bandwagon.

"I'll have the blue cheese burger and fries," Max said, "but leave out the blue cheese."

Vy let out a huff of impatience. "Why not just order a different burger if you don't want blue cheese?"

"Because you don't have a plain, normal burger on the menu!" Max countered. "All of them have something weird in them. What's wrong with plain ground steak?"

Vy sighed. "I'll tell Will to throw together a burger with absolutely nothing in it but beef. One of these days you're going to have to try something different, Max."

"Why? I like what I like."

Vy walked away without further comment.

Max felt the man's eyes on her. *So help me, God, if he starts to flirt with me, I'm going to have to set him straight in no uncertain terms.*

But no, when she met his gaze, there wasn't an ounce of playfulness in his sober stare. Of course not. He reserved that for girlie women.

Whoa, slow down, Max. You can't have it both ways.

If you want this to be strictly a business relationship, you have to be happy that he isn't flirting. Behave like a professional. Apparently he is.

Speaking of business, time to get down to it.

"You're late." *Way to go, Max. On the offensive the second the guy gets here.*

He checked his watch. "It's seven after noon now, which means I walked in here only three minutes behind schedule. Hardly enough to be termed late."

"It is in my world."

"I slowed down to look at the amusement park. It looks good."

The light bulb of his personality had been dimmed by Max's sparse welcome and she felt bad about that. She didn't know the man. She shouldn't rush to judgment. On the other hand, he could turn heads. And he did. And she didn't want him to.

The fair and rodeo were serious business.

She needed him to have his mind firmly in the game.

Max sensed the women in the restaurant taking surreptitious glimpses of Dusty.

She hoped this wasn't going to turn out to be a mistake, but what should she have done when she was hunting around the rodeo network for help? Asked for photographs?

Dusty Lincoln had come highly recommended, so highly that she hadn't had an inkling of doubt.

So here he was and she would have to make the best of it. She picked up the thread of the conversation.

"The revival committee here in Rodeo has put a good effort into bringing our park back to life. We're all set to host a comeback fair mid-August. It'll last two weeks, and the main event will be the rodeo on closing weekend. The only thing that remains is for that to take place and for us to make it a success."

"The rides look great, what I saw of them, at any rate." Dusty unwrapped his cutlery and laid his serviette across his lap, impressing Max. Good manners.

"What do you want to happen with the rodeo?" he asked. "What do you need me to organize? We'll do the usual events and culminate with the bull riding."

Max drew a breath to respond. She had hoped to at least have her lunch before getting into trouble.

At that moment the front door opened and her friend Nadine stepped into the diner.

When she saw Max, her face lit up. Newly in love with a local rancher who happened to paint the prettiest landscapes around, Nadine smiled a lot these days.

Nice to see. She'd had a run of bad luck before that.

"Hey, Max." Nadine approached. "I never see you in here midweek. What's up?" She glanced across the table, spotted Dusty and did a double take.

"Well, hey, we haven't met. I'm Nadine Campbell."

Dusty stood and shook her hand. The guy was chock-full of good manners.

"Well, hey, yourself," he said. "I'm Dusty Lincoln."

Again there passed between them that mutual-attraction thing. Again Max didn't know how that happened and how they conveyed the message about being available…or not.

"Dusty Lincoln? Your reputation precedes you," Nadine said. "I'm the local reporter. I'd love to do an interview if you have time today."

"He can't."

Both of them turned to Max and stared.

"Wish I could invite you to join us, Nadine, but we've got some…things to discuss," she finished quickly, before Nadine discovered the truth and took Max to task as Vy had. She didn't have the time right now.

"No problem, Max. Dusty, it was nice meeting you." Nadine's stunning smile dazzled.

"How's Zach?" Max asked loudly.

Nadine slid an amused grin at her. She knew exactly what Max was doing. When she held out her left hand, it alleviated all of Max's anxieties. On the third finger sat the sweetest little diamond.

"Zach is perfect," Nadine said and blushed in a way she hadn't with Dusty a moment ago.

Nadine studied Max for a moment. Her expression became crafty. She knew something was up with Max.

Nadine was a good reporter—and now editor of the only local paper—because not much got past her.

She turned to Dusty, who had remained standing. "Please, sit. I won't disturb you much longer. What brings you to Rodeo?"

"I'll be helping Max to put together the rodeo."

Nadine's face went blank. "You will?"

Might as well lay it all out there. "I hired him," Max said, in a tone of defiance mixed with false bravado.

Nadine took hold of Max's elbow and all but hauled her out of the booth. "Would you excuse us?" she tossed at Dusty.

In Vy's office down the back hallway, Nadine closed the door. "Spill," she ordered. "What's going on? At last week's committee meeting, no one said a word about hiring anyone. We don't have money."

"I know that." Max repeated what she'd told Vy was going to happen.

Nadine groaned. "You are supposed to pass all big financial decisions by the entire committee, not go Rambo on us."

Max shoved her hands into her pockets. Tension settled in her shoulders. "I didn't tell you because I knew you would all say no."

"Rightly so. There are no guarantees we'll break even, let alone make a profit."

"I'll take responsibility for this cost if I have to."

"You can't afford to do that."

"I know." The thought worried the spit out of Max. She barely broke even on the ranch, let alone thinking of paying someone else's salary for a month. Sweat dampened her armpits.

Nadine slammed her hands onto her hips. "Maybe this guy can convince you to change your ridiculous plans for the rodeo."

"No!" Max rubbed her forehead. "This can work, Nadine. It can be new and fresh and exciting. I know it can."

"But—"

Max stopped her with one upraised hand.

"Nadine, I'm so…tired." The breath whooshed out of her. She'd been fighting too many battles on her own for too long. "I'm tired of the responsibility of running a ranch nearly alone. I'm sick to death of not having time for my son."

She rubbed the spot throbbing between her eyes. "Organizing this rodeo has been a headache, but also a bright spot in my life. Before I had Josh, rodeo was my life. I have ideas that are weird, yes, but they can work. I need to be given a chance. I want to be part of this revival committee. I really do. I love all of you guys like sisters."

Still hard-edged and militant, Nadine said, "We can out-vote you on your ideas. You understand that, don't you?"

"But so far you haven't, so you must think at least something's going to work." Max sighed. "I need help and support, not criticism. I need this rodeo guy to take on some of the work."

Nadine's expression softened. "I hope this works out for you." She gestured over her shoulder toward the dining room. "What are his credentials? I know he wins rodeos, but that doesn't mean he can run one."

"Over the past decade, he's helped to organize a number of rodeos. He's got a great reputation and comes highly recommended."

"Let's hope he can help us to bring in money."

"You and me both," Max whispered fervently.

"He should be easy to work with. He has a sweet smile."

"A cocky grin, you mean."

Nadine frowned. "No. That wasn't what I saw."

Max shrugged. Nadine was welcome to her delusions. "Listen, I have an idea for an article that I need you to write. It would be great promotion for the rodeo."

Nadine perked up. "Sure. What is it?"

"I'll call you about it later. I should get back to Dusty."

Before leaving the room, Nadine hesitated and then touched Max's arm. "We all love you, Max. You know that, right?"

"Jeez, Nadine, why so heavy? Of course, we all love each other."

Max moved into Nadine's quick hug. Nadine just about squeezed the breath out of Max before following her out of the office.

In the dining room, Nadine detoured to sit with a couple of local ranchers. She must be doing a story about them.

Two women in their early twenties, a couple of the younger women in town to whom Max didn't pay much attention, stood talking to Dusty. Well, maybe not talking as much as giggling.

Max and these women lived different lives. At twenty-eight, she was only a bit older than these girls, but her life experience exceeded theirs by miles.

At their age, she'd already been a single mother to a toddler and taken on a mortgage so she could own the ranch she lived on.

The women giggled some more and placed paper servi-ettes onto the table in front of Dusty.

"We saw your win in Colorado on the weekend. You were amazing."

"Thanks." Okay, so maybe his smile was a bit sweet. He signed the paper slips graciously.

Max got angry. She needed his focus centered on the rodeo, not on the local beauties.

The girls walked away with tiny flirtatious waves of their fingers and oh-so-sexy struts.

Dear God, they made Max feel old.

"I sure hope you're planning to work here as well as flirt."

The smile dropped from his face. "I was being polite. I didn't approach them. They approached me. Should I have ignored them?"

"Do you get asked for autographs often?"

"Often enough," he said. Still unsmiling, he went on, "Let's get back to business. About the rodeo. We'll have all of the usual events, and finish the weekend with bull riding at the end."

"No."

"No? But bull riding's the big draw. You never start with it. We always want it at the end for a big finish."

Max girded her proverbial loins against his reaction. She knew in her bones this wasn't going to go well. The whole town already thought she was foolhardy. "No bull riding."

He fell back against the banquette, mouth open.

"No—" He swallowed and started again. "No bull rid-ing? What do you mean?"

"Exactly that. It's cruel. I won't have it in my rodeo."

His jawline, already impressive in its jutting manliness, hardened.

"You can't have a rodeo without bull riding. It's a big-ticket event. *The* event. It brings in money and the best rodeo stars."

"I can make this rodeo bring in money anyway."

"You sure about that?"

She shot him a confident nod. No sense letting him know how much sleep she lost every night because of her unusual decision. Bucking rodeo tradition wasn't easy in Western culture.

"We'll make money," she insisted.

She sensed Dusty giving himself time to bring his shock and anger under control.

"I've never heard of something this— I've never heard of a decision like this about the rodeo."

He'd probably meant to say "something this idiotic or stupid."

"*How* do you intend to make money without bull riding?" he asked.

The thumping of her pulse overrode the beat of the music on the radio. She *knew* what his reaction was going to be. "Polo."

His blank stare unnerved her. Those eyes were too deep with intelligence, the lashes fringing them too long, making his beauty hard to take.

The look he regarded her with throbbed with both dissatisfaction and disbelief.

"What did you say?" he asked, putting a finger behind one ear and pushing the lobe forward. "I don't think I heard you right."

"You did. I plan to put on a polo match."

"*Polo?*" he asked, voice loud enough to draw the attention of half the diners. "At a *rodeo?*"

Vy plunked down two full dinner plates onto the table.

"Talk some sense into her, would you?" Vy said to Dusty. "The committee has gotten nowhere arguing with her."

Max shot Vy a look that said *traitor*.

Vy shot her a "what do you expect?" frown and strode away.

Only one person in this entire town understood and agreed with Max on this issue, and that man was Vy's husband. In truth polo had been his idea originally. Vy rode him just as hard about the issue as she rode Max.

Now here was opposition from the hired help, too.

She scrubbed her face. Her hands smelled like flowers from Vy's cream. Her fatigue made her cranky. What else was new? She'd been tired for years. Ergo, she'd been cranky for a long time.

"Okay, listen," she said, leaning forward. "Ever since we decided to revive the fair and rodeo and I took over the rodeo organization, I've studied rodeos all over this land."

He nodded for her to continue.

"It's the same everywhere. Everywhere. Nothing changes. All of the same events in all of the same order."

"So?"

"So why would anyone come out to Rodeo, Montana, to see all of the same things they can see anywhere else? Why not just go to…to…Kalamazoo like they do every year?"

Dusty frowned. "There's no rodeo in Kalamazoo."

She slammed a hand onto the table and set cutlery jumping. "I know that! I just put out a name to make a point." She felt the eyes of half of the restaurant patrons on her, most of them leaning forward to eavesdrop better.

With an effort, she calmed herself. "My point is that we need something different, something truly original, to pull in the kinds of crowds we'll require to make this entire venture financially viable.

"There is no arguing against this. It's a done deal. Many

of the arrangements have already been made. It's only a matter now of finalizing everything."

"Then why do you need me?"

"I'm overworked. I have a million and one details to take care of and not enough time."

She picked up her burger and bit into it, delish just the way it was without weird crap inside.

She chewed and swallowed.

"You must have a good network. I need you to convince all the rodeo riders who you know that they have to be involved in this rodeo."

He picked up his knife and fork slowly, his mouth still hanging open a little in shock. "You still plan to have some traditional rodeo events?"

She nodded and bit into her burger again. Giving him time to think, she chewed and wiped her fingers on her serviette.

"Do you want the job or don't you?" she asked, her tone almost belligerent. God help her, she was sick of resistance.

Irritation flowed from the man in waves. He'd clapped his mouth shut and looked like he was physically chewing on the problem. He thought about it for a while before answering. "I want it."

Max couldn't afford to let either her surprise or her relief show.

"Good. Looks like we might get along," she said. "After lunch, follow me out to my ranch and I'll show you where you'll be staying."

For the rest of the meal, they ate in silence, neither one of them invested in trying to make small talk.

Max didn't have a speck of the social skills that other women used to get by in life. Idle conversation had always seemed like a waste of time to her. She just didn't know how to do it.

Dusty Lincoln was either pissed off or looking to come to terms with her deviation from a normal rodeo.

Michael Moreno stepped into the diner with his two children as well as his new wife's two kids. Samantha, his wife and the revival committee's accountant, was not with him, thank God.

When Samantha heard that Max had hired an employee, she would hit the roof.

Max couldn't take any more criticism today.

And she had the feeling the argument about bull riding wasn't over with Dusty.

Michael said hi as he passed, but did a double take when he recognized Dusty.

There was an awful lot of double-taking in the diner today. Dusty was a bigger celebrity than Max had guessed, but she'd been away from the rodeo for too many years.

Michael and Dusty shook hands.

"Saw you ride Cyclone a couple of years ago," Michael said.

Dusty leaned back in the booth, a confident man satisfied with his reputation. "He was about as bad a bull as I've ever ridden."

"You did a great job." Michael turned his attention to Max. "Are you sure you won't reconsider—"

"Don't go there, Michael."

Moreno, as well as the rest of the local ranchers, did not agree with Max's decision.

He backed off. "I guess if the revival committee can't convince you to keep bull riding on the agenda, nothing I say will make a difference."

He and Dusty exchanged commiserating smiles before Michael left to find a booth for himself and his kids.

Cripes. Not only women fell under Dusty's spell. So did men.

She'd heard a lot about Dusty. He lived a charmed life. Max did not. In fact, her life proved harder day by day. When would she catch a break?

If she could convince Dusty of the rightness of doing something unusual at the newly revived Rodeo, Montana, rodeo and fair, they just might be successful and bring in a crowd for curiosity's sake alone.

She *had* done her research. Plenty of it.

She had ideas that sounded strange, but she thought they could bring in good money for the fair…if only people would trust her.

And maybe horses would fly and somebody somewhere would decree there were thirty hours in the day instead of only twenty-four.

What difference would that make? Life would find a way to overschedule those hours, too.

Dusty chowed down on his meal, ignoring her and offering smiles to Vy and any other woman who passed the table.

He had nothing even vaguely resembling sweetness for Max, but what did she expect? She'd just burst his rodeo balloon.

Max paid for lunch, tossed her serviette on the table and stood.

"Let's go out to my ranch and get you settled in."

Chapter 2

Life was not so good.

How had he let his father talk him into this?

He had better things to do with his time than to become involved in ventures doomed to fail.

A polo match? At a *rodeo*?

He'd thought it would be a piece of cake to come to town and charm this woman with the ridiculous idea out of her... ridiculous idea.

But Maxine Porter was not charmable, if such a word existed.

Dusty followed Max out to her ranch, her pickup truck well broken in and maybe even just this side of giving up the ghost.

Her revelation about the rodeo almost had him driving right past the turnoff to her ranch and moving on to wherever common sense still existed in this world.

No bull riding.

Who ever heard of such a thing?

Dumb, dumb, dumb idea. He couldn't wrap his head around it.

One of Dwight Yoakam's old hits came on the radio. "It Won't Hurt."

Oh, yeah, it sure would. Canceling bull riding could kill her rodeo before it even got off the ground.

With a flick of his wrist he turned off the radio, no longer in the mood for music.

Worse, she was replacing it with a *polo match*.

So that was the weird event that had his dad's friend so worried. With good reason!

No one wanted polo at a rodeo. Period.

How was he supposed to convince this woman not to do it?

His nerves beat a frantic tattoo.

Slowing so he wouldn't disturb Thunder on the turn onto the driveway, he pulled up behind Max's truck in a yard that was as neat as a pin, in front of a house that had seen better days.

The stables were in good repair—obviously where the money went in this operation.

Her ranch. No husband? No significant other? A ranch was a lot of responsibility for one person.

She certainly *looked* like she spent all her time working. He doubted he'd ever seen a more mannish woman. Sure, he understood that looks weren't everything, but men noticed anyway.

Not that it meant much to him. For some reason, clothes never had.

He liked women in all forms, but this one seemed to be doing everything in her power to deny her own femininity.

Her black hair had been cut short—hacked off would be more accurate—without any style.

Same with her clothes. An oversize man's plaid shirt hid what shape her body might have. She'd tucked it into a pair of baggy jeans that hung low on her hips. An unadorned brown leather belt held them up.

Cowboy boots as old as the Alamo proclaimed her a working woman.

She jammed an ancient cowboy hat onto her head. Looked like she'd been using it for years judging by the salt stains where the brim met the crown.

The old brim, which hid her freckled face from the world, looked like it might have been nibbled on by a mouse or two.

Most women had more vanity. Curious.

Dusty moved to get out of his truck, but she motioned him back in and climbed into the passenger seat.

"See that house?" That voice, though. It was downright sultry—low and husky—and seemed out of place coming from her. She pointed to a small bungalow in the near distance.

He nodded.

"That's where you'll be staying. Drive over."

Dusty parked in front of a tidy house in better shape than the main house. Pots of red geraniums lined the steps up to a small veranda with one white wicker armchair. Used often, a blue-and-white cushion had the distinct impression of someone's ass in it.

A smaller chair sat beside the big one. A kid's?

Again, curious.

He stepped out of the truck and his left leg buckled. Hissing, he maneuvered his foot securely under his knee and stood.

Damned knee was not going to act up. He wouldn't allow it.

One way or another, he was going to make sure they went ahead with a bull-riding event and he was goddamned going to win it.

As far as he could tell, the only person who wanted a polo match was this woman. Everyone else in town seemed to want bull riding on the menu.

He sure as hell did. Taking this job meant he wouldn't participate in other rodeo events this month. The salary from the rodeo committee made up for that, but he wouldn't turn down the chance for another win this season.

He dragged his bags out of the back of the truck.

Max opened the unlocked front door.

Dusty followed her inside. The living room looked as cozy and clean as the outside of the house.

Comfortable old furniture ranged around the room. Ranching magazines and popular mystery novels sat on a coffee table.

A smoke-tinged hearth anchored the far wall.

Max led him down the hallway to a bedroom at the back, bypassing a much larger bedroom.

"I can't have the big room?"

"That belongs to Marvin. This is his house. While you're here, he'll be staying in the main house."

"Marvin? Is he the foreman here?" Dusty knew full well who Marvin was, but he had a charade to keep up.

"Sure" was the extent of her response.

Why not just say yes?

"I'd rather you didn't use his room," she said. "It has all of his stuff in it. There's no point in moving it out for only one month. You have free rein with the rest of the house." She pointed across the hallway. "Laundry room."

He dropped his two bags onto the bed and followed her to a small, clean kitchen.

"Here's the coffee machine. Marvin filled the fridge with food. We didn't know what you'd like so it's basic. You've got sandwich meats from the deli and fresh bread, along with some of Vy's potato salad and a lemon meringue pie."

"Lemon meringue is my favorite. How'd ya guess?"

She didn't smile or laugh. The woman could suck all of the warmth out of a sunny day.

"Is there a grill anywhere?" he asked.

"Marvin has one out behind the house."

"I'll pick up steaks and frozen burgers later."

She nodded and led him out of the house. "Let's go. I'll introduce you to the horses. Marvin, too, if he's around."

Dusty climbed into his truck and reversed the trailer to the side of the stable. Around back, he eased Thunder out.

Inside the stable, they found Marvin with a young boy Dusty guessed to be eight or so.

Marvin was an older man past retirement age. Over the years, Dusty had met him occasionally when he visited Dad, but he hadn't seen him for a few years, not since Dusty took to the rodeo circuit.

The man had aged since the last time Dusty had seen him.

They shook hands, pretending they didn't know each other.

Max made the introductions with her hands resting on the kid's shoulders. The boy's name was Josh.

"Gramps is taking me out riding," the boy said.

Marvin had only ever had a son, if Dusty's recollection was correct. So Max must be his daughter-in-law?

Josh looked up at Max with a wistful, yearning expression. "Mom, will you come?"

She ran her fingers through his hair in an affectionate manner out of sorts with her gruff exterior.

"Okay," she said and Josh's face lit with a huge grin.

Josh turned to Dusty. "Want to come see our ranch?"

About to nod the okay, Dusty startled when Max said, "Not today, Josh. He'll want to settle in and get unpacked."

Unpack a duffel bag? He moved so often he had his systems down pat. It would take him all of ten minutes.

He didn't like how controlling this woman was.

She turned away as though dismissing him.

It got his dander up.

"I can unpack later," Dusty said and had the satisfaction of seeing her frown.

"Really, you must be tired," she said. "You don't have to ride out with us."

"I'd like to see the ranch." Some little devil sitting on his shoulder wanted to get under her skin for making his life difficult. No bull riding. A polo match. Plus, she didn't seem to like him. She hadn't from the moment he'd stepped into the diner in town.

Tough. He was who he was.

"You won't be working on the ranch," she said, still arguing to get her way, dammit. "You'll be working in the office in the house, organizing the rodeo."

She obviously didn't want to spend any more time with him than she had to. She'd made her unfounded judgments of him in the restaurant.

"But, Mom," the boy said, "I want to show Dusty the land."

To Dusty, he boasted, "Someday, it's going to be my ranch." Dusty liked the kid's pride.

"I'd love to come along for the ride," Dusty said, yet again thwarting the woman. "Give me a couple of minutes to get Thunder settled into a stall."

The nod of capitulation Max granted him in the face of her son's desire was about as ungracious as anything Dusty had ever seen. He turned away to lead Thunder to the stall Marvin indicated, a grin splitting his face because it was fun to prick at her surliness.

Immature, Dusty.

Unrepentant, Dusty responded to his conscience, *Yeah, but fun.*

"Give your horse a break from the drive here." Marvin opened the door to the empty stall. "Use one of Max's horses. This here is Pegasus. She'll give you a good ride."

Dusty settled Thunder with water and feed, letting Max's boy run around and help him.

Cute kid. Eager.

They saddled three horses for the adults and a pony for the boy. Josh had long legs. He'd need a bigger horse soon.

Max's horses were in fine shape, well cared for.

They rode for an hour while Josh shared everything there was to know about his mother's ranch.

Max stopped and watched cattle for a while. She rode up beside a steer, dismounted and picked up a rear hoof.

"Marvin, looks like we've got a problem here. You want to separate him from the herd and take him back?"

"Sure. I'll call the vet."

"Take a good look in the barn. It might be something we can handle ourselves."

They should have a vet look anyway, in Dusty's opinion. He didn't take chances with animals, but the more he saw of the place, the more he thought finances might be an issue.

The boy stayed to help Marvin while Dusty rode back with Max. They rode in an uncomfortable silence. Dusty liked to talk.

She didn't.

He didn't know what to make of her lack of friendliness. Women usually liked him.

What had he done to her other than show up to help out with her rodeo?

Back in the stable, they tended to the horses, dividing up the work fairly, still in silence.

From the corner of his eye, he studied Max and came to the conclusion that she wasn't freezing him out. With the serious frown on her forehead, he thought maybe she was worried about something and only barely aware of him.

When his phone rang and she startled, he realized she'd been so far into her thoughts that she'd forgotten all about him.

It didn't happen often that a woman forgot about Dusty Lincoln's presence.

Not vanity. Just fact.

His phone sounded different. He took it out of his shirt pocket.

Beyoncé's "Single Ladies."

What the— Where had that come from? It wasn't his ringtone.

He checked the incoming call.

His mom. It figured. Somehow she'd gotten hold of his phone and programmed Beyoncé to ring when she called.

When had she done it? He remembered that she'd attended the rodeo on the weekend to watch him ride and had held his stuff for him. The bigger question was how had she known his password to get in and change things?

Yet again, she had proved herself to be all-powerful and all-knowing. He had to smile.

Beyoncé sang on. *Oh, Mom.* The song was her idea of a joke.

She thought Dusty had too many women in his life and needed to find one to marry.

She'd been pestering him since he'd turned thirty over a year ago to find a girl and settle down. Why should he? He was having fun. No need to put a ring on any woman's finger just yet.

Besides, he'd have to find the right woman first and how could he make a choice? He liked them all.

Except maybe Maxine Porter. He sobered.

His phone still chirped.

"Excuse me," he said. "I have to take this." If he didn't, Mom would just call back in five minutes.

He turned away and answered the phone. "Hello?"

"No 'Hi, Mom'?" His mother laughed on the other end of the line. She knew he must be with a woman or he would have answered, "Hi, Mom."

"What's up?" he asked.

"Just calling to remind you about the family picnic next weekend. All of your aunts, uncles and cousins can make it this year."

Dusty bit back an oath. Somehow she was meddling again. Did she have some new woman to introduce him to? "I can't come. I already told you I'd be busy."

"But you're the star of the family. You're why I'm having the picnic and why the family is coming."

Sometimes Dusty resented his family's intrusion in his life. Yes, he was his parents' miracle baby and only child, the one they'd given up hope of ever having, and the youngest of all of his cousins, but being called the star of the family embarrassed him.

Hanging on to his patience, he said, "I already told you I'd be busy." He loved his mother, but she exasperated him at times. "Why did you plan it anyway?"

"Because there aren't any rodeos booked for next weekend as far as I know. You know I follow them all."

True. Mom was his biggest fan.

"It's not a rodeo. It's a job."

"A real job?" His mother sounded hopeful, but the implied insult rankled.

"The job Dad set me up with, remember?" He kept his voice low so Max wouldn't hear that tidbit.

"Oh, that's right. It's temporary, though."

He fought to keep his voice even. "But bull riding is a real job, just so we're clear."

"For how much longer? What happens when you get too old for it? What happens if you get injured again?"

Mention of injuries was not allowed. His knee was all healed, it *was*, and he could still ride.

"Hey, you know that word is taboo."

"Which one?"

"The one that starts with the letter *i*."

"I know, Dusty, but I worry. Now, about this job of yours with Marvin…can it become permanent?"

Dusty moaned. Not again. Always with the "find a good

woman and get a secure job and settle down" business. "Can we have this discussion another time?"

"Sure, honey. I'll call tomorrow."

Dusty bit back a cutting remark. He didn't sass his mom. It seemed that tomorrow they would have the exact same conversation as today. He loved his mother, but sometimes...

"Don't forget about the picnic. I'm sure you can take one Saturday off." After that parting shot, she cut the connection.

With an inward groan, he stuffed his phone into his pocket.

Even though he loved his family, they overwhelmed him. He'd been the miracle baby, coming along long after his parents and their extended families had given up hope of them getting pregnant.

His childhood had been happy. He'd been indulged by his parents and his many aunts and uncles and all of his many older cousins.

How lucky could one guy be?

Yeah, he was lucky. Even so, his huge, loving, benevolent family stifled him.

Sometimes he needed to spend time alone.

Max watched him, a curious frown on her forehead.

He realized he'd been staring at his phone for a protracted time.

"Sorry about that," he said, unwilling to satisfy her curiosity and feed the small-town gossip mill. He had no idea if she was the kind of woman to spread rumors, but he didn't take chances in a town he didn't know.

"No problem," she said.

He watched her strong arms curry her horse. She didn't cut corners. Her horses bore signs of being pampered.

He approved.

"Can I ask you something?" He finished dealing with the horse he'd ridden.

She looked wary. "What?"

Why the distrust? What did she think he was after?

"Where did you get this idea for a polo match?" If he could find out where it started and argue coherently, maybe he could change her mind before it was too late.

"From Vy's husband," she said.

"Vy? From the diner? But she doesn't approve." He sounded bewildered because he was.

"No. She doesn't."

Already he knew Max wasn't going to give in on this. She sounded firmly entrenched. But it was unconscionable to add to the rodeo an event guaranteed to fail.

He had to give his arguments a shot.

"Bull riding draws more income and sponsorship than any other rodeo event."

Knowing everything there was to know about the rodeo, he cited statistics.

"It's the most exciting eight seconds in the rodeo."

"It's the most dangerous eight seconds on the planet and it should be banned for all time. Men have been killed. Worse, they've lived diminished lives because of damage from concussions. Is that truly your way to go?"

"It's my life!" Dusty exploded. "It's every bull rider's personal decision. We're grown men and capable of making our own choices."

"True. I don't dispute that. But *this* decision about *this* rodeo is mine, not yours. There will be no bull riding."

He argued. He pled.

She didn't budge. She got tight in the jaw.

Then and there, he decided his next step would be to talk to the guy who'd started it all, the one who'd given Max the flaky idea.

She'd hired Dusty to make this rodeo a success. He wasn't in the habit of failing.

"Can I talk to him?" he asked.

"Who?"

"Vy's husband."

For an instant, her shoulders tensed. Maybe he'd insulted her. Surely he had. In her position, he would have felt the insult, but she relaxed and shrugged.

"You're not ready to give up, are you?" she asked.

"Nope," he answered.

"Let's go." She fished her truck keys out of her pocket.

"We can take my truck," he said. "It's a more reliable vehicle."

She stiffened. "Nope. We're good in my truck."

She likes to have her own way. Didn't bode well for their working together.

He worried more now, not just about the lack of bull riding, but because Max had to have control.

Women liked him because he was an easygoing guy, but he could be pushed too far.

Ten minutes later, they turned onto the fairgrounds, surprising Dusty.

"He lives here?"

"Yes. He's the original owner's grandson. We're going to that big old brick house at the back of the grounds."

Dusty twisted his head in every direction, taking it all in. "I've never seen such beautiful rides at a fairground."

A smile turned up the corners of her lips. "Thanks. You know Nadine, who you met at the diner?"

Dusty smiled, remembering drop-dead gorgeous Nadine with the stunning red hair, vibrant green eyes and flawless skin.

"What about her?" he asked.

"Her soon-to-be husband painted all of the rides. Look at those teacups."

She pointed and he craned his neck.

"Beautiful. Whimsical." He stared until it was out of sight. "It's like something straight out of *Alice in Wonderland.*"

"Yeah, it is," she answered, drawing Dusty's glance because of the smile in her voice. That bit of pleasure softened her features.

"If the fair can make money on whimsy and pretty rides, you're already winning," he said. *But*, he thought, *you need to do a hell of a lot more.*

"Well, we're all doing our part," Max said. "Each of the committee members has her own role—Nadine does publicity, Vy is taking care of food and I'm in charge of the rodeo."

So that was why she had so much sway with the bull-riding decision.

They parked in front of an old two-story brick house.

At Max's knock, a guy answered the door in a pale pink button-down shirt, beige chinos and tasseled loafers, a man so far out of his element here in rural Montana he should be uncomfortable.

He wasn't. He smiled and extended a hand when Max introduced Dusty and stated the reason for their visit. A firm handshake belied the softness Dusty had assumed would be part of his character.

"I met your wife earlier," Dusty said. "Hell of a cook." He wouldn't have thought the beautiful diner owner with the bountiful body would go for a man was as refined as Sam Carmichael. On the way over, Max mentioned that he hailed from Manhattan, a Wall Street businessman before moving to Rodeo.

When Sam caught Dusty giving him the once-over, he grinned and seemed to read Dusty's mind.

"Yeah, I know," Sam said. "Vy could have picked one of the local cowboys but she didn't. She had years to choose any one of you, but she waited for me to come to town. I snapped her up. The rest of you losers can go weep."

Dusty laughed. "No accounting for taste," he said, and Sam responded with a laugh of his own. Solid sense of humor.

"Come on in and sit down." Sam led the way into a comfortable living room that had seen better days. All of the furniture had been broken in.

An old man slept in an armchair beside the fireplace.

Max sat in the chair beside him, pulled an afghan from the back of her armchair and covered the man with it, her action affectionate.

Dusty wouldn't have taken her for the nurturing type.

He knew better than to give in to first impressions, but he was human and as judgmental as the average person. And she had been nothing but prickly with Dusty.

"This is Sam's grandfather Carson," Max said, not really an introduction, as the man snoozed on. "Carson's father started the rodeo and amusement park nearly a hundred years ago."

Dusty sat on the sofa and leaned back. Sam sat on the hearth on his grandfather's other side. He offered them tea or coffee, but they declined.

"Tell me about the polo match," Dusty said, anxious to get to the point of the visit. "Why at a rodeo?"

"I heard that Max didn't want to do a traditional rodeo," Sam said. "Back in New York I belonged to an amateur polo league." He settled his arms onto his knees. "I know you won't believe me, but polo matches are incredibly fast-paced and exciting. I told Max she should do it. When she balked—"

Dusty's surprise must have shown because Sam continued, "Yes, she balked, just like you're doing. She changed her mind when I told her my friends and I would cover all the costs and would even contribute a prize for the winning team. It's a win-win. Neither the fair committee nor the town will put out money for the event."

Okay, so it wasn't a gamble to mount the match since it wouldn't cost the town anything, but neither would it bring in money if the crowds wouldn't come out for it.

The costs of putting on a normal rodeo, including a bull-riding event, were high, and you had to believe that ticket sales would offset those costs.

On the other hand, there was still no advantage for local cowboys who depended on the rodeo circuit for a certain amount of income. "What good does it do the locals if the money goes right back to one of the teams from New York?"

"One of the teams? Max didn't tell you all of it?"

"He didn't give me a chance," Max grumbled. She slouched low in the armchair and held Carson's hand. Every so often, she checked to make sure he was okay, pulling the blanket higher about his chest, the gesture so sweet and affectionate it shocked Dusty. No reason why it should have. He didn't know the woman.

"He just took offense and wanted to talk to you," Max, the tattletale, continued.

"That's never stopped you before from making your opinions known," Sam said, the sentiment hostile, but his tone friendly.

An infinitesimal smile flickered across Max's lips, here and gone in an instant. She could be teased and she could like it.

Dusty filed that away for future use. He liked teasing women. He liked charming them. Hell, he just liked being with them, pure and simple.

"What's the rest of the idea that Max didn't tell me?" he asked.

"Only one of the teams will be me and my friends from New York."

"Where are the others coming from? London?" He racked his brain for what little he knew about polo. "South America? I still don't see how that's going to appeal to anyone coming to a fair and rodeo here in Montana."

"The other team will be you."

"Me?"

"You and all of your bull-riding, bronc-riding and barrel-racing buddies."

Stunned, Dusty couldn't speak for a moment. "You want rodeo cowboys to play polo?"

"We want you to participate in a polo match, yes."

Dusty stared at Sam. "A bunch of cowboys playing polo? You have to be kidding."

"Nope," Sam said. "Not one iota."

Dusty's gaze slid between Sam and Max, who both watched him placidly. "But that's…that's…just plain unheard of."

"Yes, but if you study it from a bunch of different angles—" Sam held up one finger to forestall arguments "—it's actually a damned good idea."

"How so?" Dusty knew he sounded sulky, but come on. In what universe did polo at a rodeo make any sense?

"You might not think so, but polo is tough and cutthroat," Sam said.

Dusty hadn't been thinking that. He turned to Max.

She nodded. "Sam showed me films of their matches." She glanced at Sam and smiled a little meanly. "He's tougher than he looks."

Sam took no offense. "It might seem like a rodeo audience won't be interested, but it's a riveting spectator sport, on top of being competitive and strategic, like any other rodeo event."

"What I had actually been thinking," Dusty interrupted, "was that the city guys have the advantage. Rodeo riders are a tough, competitive lot, true, but they have no experience with polo. How are we supposed to win?"

"With practice."

"The rodeo is less than a month away. How are we supposed to practice?"

"My friends are bringing ponies in by the end of the week. You can get your buddies together to practice on them." Sam smiled. "It might not be their best ponies, though. They'll likely save the best for themselves. You might want to train on your own horses."

"Ponies?"

"They're not really ponies, Dusty," Max said. "They're only called that. They're actually full-size horses. And they are gorgeous."

"That's right," Sam said. "The term *ponies* is in reference to how agile they are, not to their size."

Dusty nodded. Okay, but… "These city guys are too competitive to lend us their best?"

"Too protective. These are their babies."

"Seriously?"

Sam stared. "How do you feel about your horse?"

Dusty got Sam's point. "Protective."

"Right. These owners have put out big bucks on these ponies. Serious money. Don't worry. Their second-best ponies are spectacular. You'll be impressed."

"You honestly think a bunch of city slickers and their game will engage a rural audience?" Dusty asked, not sure which one of them he was directing the question to. Max knew the West and Sam knew polo.

Max glanced at Sam before checking her no-frills, no-

nonsense watch. "You want to put on one of the videos for him? We can't stay long. Maybe twenty more minutes. Marvin's probably got dinner started by now."

Sam stood and turned on the TV on a stand at the far end of the room. He put a DVD into a player on a shelf underneath the television and fast-forwarded.

"Here's last year's final match, coming down to the wire. Watch how the ponies move."

For the next ten minutes, Dusty watched and marveled. Sam was right. The players worked hard. The ponies worked harder. The men maneuvered their animals about as well as anyone barrel racing in a tournament or rounding up cattle on the range.

Tension glistened in the sweat on the riders' faces and hardened their shoulders and arms. The agile, quick ponies were, in a word, fabulous. He wanted to ride one.

When the match ended, Sam turned off the machine and raised his eyebrows at Dusty.

"Well?"

"Well." He gave both of them his attention. "It's exciting. It's fast-paced. It's tough."

Sam smiled. Max looked satisfied.

Dusty might not like the idea of polo instead of bull riding, but he loved competition. That put it mildly. He could see himself trying to win against a bunch of city boys.

"But…" Dusty said and they grew serious. "We need more than this."

"I was thinking—"

"Max, don't even mention it." Sam had turned stern, all hints of teasing gone.

"But—"

"No!"

Sam's anger surprised Dusty. Dusty had pegged him for an easygoing guy.

"What are you guys fighting about?" He glanced from one to the other.

"You don't want to know," Sam said, expression unforgiving.

Face every bit as hard-edged, Max shook her head.

Into the tense silence, Dusty inserted, "I have an idea."

"What?" they both asked, one as unhappy as the other.

Dusty had grown up in a home in which fighting and tension didn't exist. He might love competition, but he hated conflict.

"On second thought… You're both angry. Maybe we should wait for another time." And why was he even considering this? If he spoke his idea out loud, it would sound like support of the polo match instead of bull riding.

Sam pulled his anger under control. Max looked like she still struggled and Dusty sensed that the woman didn't give up on grudges easily.

She relented enough to say, "Go ahead. What are you thinking?"

Dusty didn't much care about their argument, so he put forth his idea. "You got these city guys coming out to compete in their own sport and all of us cowboys are just supposed to go along with it."

They nodded.

"Your point?" Sam asked.

"That bugs me. We're going all-in for the city boys. Turnabout is fair play. How about if we set up a series of competitions and the city riders have to *also* compete in *our* disciplines?"

There was nothing mean about Max's smile now. It blossomed full of pleasure. "That's what I said! I've been trying to get Sam to agree with me for months! Glad to have your voice added to mine."

Mercurial, she'd surprised Dusty again.

Grouchy one moment. Sweet the next. Her ideas were too far out. Her ideas were sound.

Dusty was having trouble keeping up.

Sam groaned. "That's what we've been fighting about. It's unfair. My guys have never participated in those kinds of sports."

"I've never been involved in polo, but you're asking it of me. If, and that's a big if, I can get any cowboys to agree to it, they'll have…what?…only a few weeks to practice? It's hardly fair."

"I know." Sam sounded glum. "Believe me, I get what you're saying, but I've already got my friends on board and willing to front the costs. I just don't know if I can get them to agree to any changes at this point, or if it'd even be fair to ask. We can't risk anyone backing out."

"Let me talk to them," Max said.

"Like you can sweet talk them into it," Sam scoffed.

"Sam, you have no idea what I'm capable of." She sounded so confident, Dusty wondered if maybe she could do it.

She might not be the least bit feminine, but she had a beautiful voice that conjured up images her face and body sure didn't deliver on. He had a feeling she could win out on stubbornness alone, but as a last resort, on the phone her voice might seduce.

"You should let her try," Dusty said.

Surprise showed on Max's face.

Sam didn't look convinced. "Seriously?"

"Why not?"

"I don't know."

"Let her give it a shot."

"Okay."

Sam took a notepad out of a drawer and wrote down a few names and numbers. He tore off a sheet and handed the paper to Max.

"Knock yourself out."

On their way out the door, Max stood close to Sam and said, "Trust me. Okay?"

Dusty didn't really like the woman's demeanor in general, or the fact that she had no give in her, but she sounded sincere.

Sam's rigid shoulders eased and he hugged her. To Dusty's shock, the woman who looked like she didn't have a soft or affectionate bone in her body hugged him back hard.

Chapter 3

Dusty ate a double-decker sandwich for dinner along with a bagged salad and frozen fries he heated in the oven.

He'd just finished washing his few dishes when someone knocked on the frame of the screen door.

"It's Marvin," a voice called. "Can I come in?"

"I'm in the kitchen." Dusty dried his hands, snagged a couple of cans of beer from the fridge and opened them.

When Marvin stepped into the kitchen, Dusty handed him one.

"Thanks," Marvin said. "How're your parents?"

"Great. Growing old gracefully with all their faculties intact. Still fit and healthy. Touch wood." He rapped his knuckles against the big round oak kitchen table.

"Let's go out on the back porch," Marvin said, leading the way. "Max won't be able to see us from the big house."

They sat in a pair of oversize aging rattan armchairs with plastic flowered cushions.

Dusty settled himself in and crossed one ankle over his other knee.

On the far side of the house, the sun set in the west, at the front where two chairs, one big and one little, looked like they were used regularly.

Back here, full dusk crept in, filling in with shadows the spaces between the trees and the low hills in the distance.

Dusty took a long pull on his beer. "Why am I here, Marvin? She's a stubborn woman. Not sure what I can do about that."

"You got to talk sense into Max or she's going to ruin the rodeo. A full-on frontal attack won't work. The whole town has already tried that. She gets defensive and digs in her heels. You got to work on her from the inside. As the one who's helping her to run the rodeo, maybe she'll listen to you."

Dusty doubted it. "How'd you get her to hire me?"

"She doesn't know that I did. She thinks she hired you to run the rodeo all on her own. She needed help. I just made sure your name made it to the top of her list."

Dusty asked, "You want to tell me what's going on? Polo replacing bull riding? Is she lacking good judgment, or what?"

"Well, now," Marvin answered. "You've got two issues conflagrated into one."

"Do you mean conflated?"

Marvin responded with a good-natured nod. "Yep. That's it. Let's separate them."

"Okay."

"She decided right from the start to cancel the bull riding and had to fill in that gap. Carson's grandson came to town and mentioned the idea of a polo match to Max, damn his hide. Now she won't get it out of her head."

"But why cancel the bull riding? That's what I don't get. Why replace it with polo?"

"With or without the polo," Marvin said, "Max wasn't going to have a bull-riding competition. No way, no how."

"Why the hell not?"

"She claims it's cuz it's cruel to the animal."

"Is she an animal activist?"

"She loves animals and cares about their welfare, but that's not the heart of the issue at all. That's not why she would cancel bull riding. Hell, if that was her concern, she'd also cancel everything else."

"True. There are plenty of rodeo events that *look* cruel."

"They look cruel," Marvin agreed with qualification in

his tone. "But I've never met a bunch of people who cared more for animals than rodeo riders."

"True again. So what's her problem?"

"My son."

Dusty knew nothing about the whys and wherefores of Marvin's son and Max.

"What about your son?"

Marvin shot him a puzzled frown. "He died in the rodeo."

It was Dusty's turn to look puzzled. "Why didn't I hear about that? I don't remember any Naismiths having died."

"His last name wasn't the same as mine. It was Foster."

"*Foster?* Joel Foster was *your* son?"

Marvin swallowed a few times and nodded.

"Oh, man, I'm sorry." Dusty had heard that Joel Foster had been killed by a bull at an event about nine years ago. That had been Marvin's son?

Despite the fact that Marvin kept in touch with his dad, Dusty didn't know much about the man, certainly not that his only son had passed. Dusty hadn't even gone to Joel Foster's funeral. Rodeo people came out for rodeo people, but he'd been holed up for days in a hotel room with a bad virus he'd caught on tour.

Somehow through the years, maybe because of the different surnames, Dusty had never connected Marvin to Joel.

"Joel was a good guy," he said. "A hell of a competitor."

"Thanks. I thought so, too." Pride rang in Marvin's voice, and rightly so. Joel had been one of the best.

"And way too young to die." Dusty remembered him in his early twenties.

Marvin nodded.

"Marvin, do you mind if I ask why you had different last names?"

"I didn't know about him at first. He was already three

years old when his mother came with him to the ranch. She'd given him her last name."

"You didn't know she was pregnant?"

"No. There was no emotional attachment between us, just a brief affair for the sex. We went our separate ways. I didn't think any more about it. You could have knocked me over with a feather when she showed up with Joel in tow."

"I'll bet."

"Anyway, she'd given Joel her last name instead of mine. He knew himself as a Foster, so I left it at that. He lived with me until his death, though, so he understood fully by then what his heritage was. This land was meant to go to him."

"Did his mother stay here to live with you?"

"Naw. She came to drop him off. Said she was too young to be tied down. Last I heard she died in a car accident. Drunk driving. I took Joel to the funeral. He mourned and then we moved on."

Dusty didn't have a clue what to say, so he turned the topic a few degrees.

"Tell me about Max. Is she from around here?"

"Yep. From a ranch on the other side of town. Her stepfather owns it now. In her mother's will, the whole thing was left to him and nothin' to Max. Wasn't the right thing to do at all."

Wow. Tough.

"Where does Max come into the equation with Joel? Was she his wife?"

"Nope. They never made it to the altar. They were young. They had a brief relationship and got pregnant. Before he left for that rodeo, they'd decided to get married for the baby's sake after he got back."

"Oh, no." Bad timing.

"She grieved for Joel, and not just because she was going

to have a baby and didn't know what to do. Her family threw her out."

"Seriously? Why? For getting pregnant?" Dusty shook his head. "Isn't that an extreme reaction in the 2000s?"

"You've never met her stepfather. Probably will in the next month somewhere around town."

"What's his problem?" Dusty set his empty can on the porch floor.

"That ain't my story to tell. Max could share it with you. Or she might not. You never know with her."

"So she came to live with you because her parents kicked her out?"

"Yep, her stepfather, and now she's buying the ranch from me. She holds the mortgage."

Dusty whistled. "That's a lot to take on."

"It is." Marvin drank some beer in the gathering darkness. "She can do it, though. She's a hard worker."

Dusty sorted through what he'd heard. "So, she doesn't want to have bull riding because it's too dangerous? Because Joel died that way?"

"Correct."

"But what about all of the riders who've survived over the years?"

Marvin finished his beer and crushed the can in his wrinkled fist. "What you got to understand about Max is how complex she is. It's taken nine years of living with her for me to finally get her. She's smart and tough. She's also emotional and sentimental. Worst of all, she's stubborn."

He picked up Dusty's can and stood. "There you go. Max in a nutshell."

Dusty followed him into the house, where Marvin deposited the cans into the recycle box.

In the front hallway, Marvin turned back and said, fervently, "You got to stop her. The committee hasn't been able to. They could outvote her on this but they won't." His voice dropped slightly. "If you knew Max, you'd know that despite the stress and all the flak she's getting, she's come alive planning this rodeo—probably reminds her of her own days on the circuit." He cracked his knuckles. "Outvoting her would be like saying we don't believe in her—and we want to, but there's so much at stake for the town if this rodeo isn't a success. Me and those women on the revival committee came up with this idea of you persuading her to change her mind. It's the most—" he hesitated, searching for a word "—*delicate* way to solve our problem. You just got to, one way or another."

With that, Marvin left.

So, the women he'd met earlier today did know he was coming, despite pretending they didn't, and they were counting on him, too. *No pressure*, Dusty thought. *None at all.*

Shortly after nine, with her son in bed and the house quiet, Max rested her forehead on her palm and closed her eyes, just for a moment.

Marvin had gone off somewhere to do his own thing.

Max wondered what her friends were doing tonight, but she didn't have to stretch her imagination much. One by one, they had each found love. They were probably cuddling with their significant others at that very moment.

The best Max could hope for tonight was to curl up with a good book for a solid ten minutes before she fell asleep over it, the biggest reason why she only read in bed. That way, she could slide under the covers at some point during the night.

How many times had she awakened at one or two to find that she'd fallen sound asleep sitting up, with her hands slack and her book on the floor or tangled in the blankets somewhere?

You sure live an exciting life, Max.

Tonight, there would be no book. She faced another three hours of work.

Her account books beckoned, but instead she phoned Nadine.

On the second ring, Nadine responded.

"Sorry to bother you." A tiny mean-spirited corner of her usually generous, now turned envious, soul thought, *Not really.* "I need to run by you the idea I told you about earlier for the newspaper."

"Go ahead. I'm intrigued."

"So there will be a polo match. That's nonnegotiable, no matter how hard the committee pushes back." Max didn't have complete control, but at this late date, who else were they going to get to run the damned thing? They wouldn't replace her.

Nadine made some kind of noncommittal sound.

"How about," Max said, "if we make it the focus of our advertising for the next month? I mean, why fight it? Why not start printing articles that say things like 'You've never seen this before in a rodeo.'"

"It's certainly a unique idea, Max, but I don't think—"

"Stop. Whatever it is you're going to say, just don't." Max pulled a long breath into her lungs. "I know I'm weird."

"Aw, Max, now you just stop." The compassion in Nadine's voice warmed Max, but she had no illusions about herself.

"I'm a woman in what is still predominantly a male industry. I don't *work* on a ranch. I *own* it. I manage it. Plus, I'm not the most feminine, agreeable person around."

Nadine laughed. "Really? I hadn't noticed."

Max smiled. "Ha, ha, ha. Anyway, the one thing I have going for me, believe it or not, is good instincts. They're telling me that we should push this totally out-of-the-box idea to the limit and it will succeed."

"I'm listening."

"The big buzzword in every business, every industry, everywhere a person turns, is *marketing*. So let's really commit to this idea of doing something outside of the ordinary and market the daylights out of it as if we're geniuses for thinking of something no one else has thought of before."

"Max, I'm good at my job, but I'm not a magician."

Nadine's role on the committee was publicity and she'd been doing a fine job, but she'd said nothing so far about the polo match. Max knew why. They'd all thought they could dissuade her.

"Given all of this, I have an idea about an article."

"Go on." A male voice rumbled in the background on the other end of the line. "I'll explain later," Nadine said to Zach, no doubt. Her new fiancé.

"Okay, this original idea started with Sam after he came to Rodeo. Why don't you write a nice, long, entertaining article about how he came to town pretending to be a cowboy—"

"And did a lousy job of it," Nadine interjected.

It took them both a while to stop laughing. The whole town had known the second he'd stepped inside of the city limits that Sam was not, and never would be, a cowboy.

"The bottom line, though, is that he won Vy's heart when no local cowboy or rancher had been able to. Write their love story, Nadine. Everyone adores a good love story."

"So true, but what does this have to do with polo and the rodeo?"

"You've already written articles about the fair's history, and about Sam's grandfather. Carson ran it for so many years. Now write about Sam. Introduce this as his idea. Play up the whole 'city boy comes to town' angle to the hilt. Then he wants to bring his polo buddies into town to compete."

"That's not a bad idea. Make it highly personal and unique to Rodeo."

"Yeah! I don't know exactly what the article would be like, but you've got great skills, Nadine. You could make this story really compelling."

"I like it. You're a bit of a genius."

Max giggled. "It's about time someone noticed."

Nadine laughed.

"There's one other thing. Once we get commitments from Western rodeo performers who are willing to try this whole polo thing, you could do a series of articles about them. Like maybe one article at a time showcasing a Western rider's background and history and juxtaposing it against a polo rider's history."

"I like that a *lot*."

The excitement in Nadine's voice got Max's juices flowing. After hanging up, she got to work with a renewed energy. By eleven, that had faded. Understandable since she'd been up since five that morning.

She needed to step away from the books for a while, so she headed out to the stable to check on the horses.

Dusty ate another sandwich before bed.

What he really wanted was a big old bag of salty chips to have with another beer.

It didn't matter how much dinner he ate, Dusty still needed his bedtime snack.

He wandered out onto the small veranda and leaned against the railing, pondering everything that had happened today.

Rodeo, Montana, and Max had presented him with too many surprises today. No, more than that. Shocks.

Tonight, with his knee aching from the long drive to town, he felt his age.

The twinges in his loose knee terrified him.

Without the rodeo, he had nothing.

It was all he'd done for two decades.

How was he supposed to give it up?

What was he supposed to do instead?

The sandwich stuck in his throat. He swallowed the last of it and wiped his hands on his jeans.

The night was warm, but not insufferably so.

This far along at the first of August, the bugs weren't bad. A bat swooped across the nearest meadow, probably keeping the population of said insects down.

A light shone in the stable, someone working late. Dusty wondered who. He hadn't seen or met any of Max's ranch hands yet.

He checked his watch. Just going on eleven thirty.

A minute later, the light went out and someone walked from the stable to the main house in a pale dusting of moonlight. Max.

Her attire might be mannish, but her walk wasn't. Here in the near darkness without being able to see her clothes, it was obvious she was a woman.

And wasn't that a weird, useless observation to make?

He never had, and never would, show interest in an employer.

She entered the main house and closed the door without a sound.

Inside, a light went on in a window on the side he was facing. It stayed on for a while.

She wasn't going to sleep yet.

He headed in to get ready for bed, scratching an itch on his throat.

His hand touched rope and beads. The necklace the

buckle bunny had given him. He'd left the last town still wearing it for her sake, only because she had the sweetest smile. He'd meant to take it off in the truck. He'd forgotten about it.

He slipped a bead through a loop at the back of the necklace and took it off. In a few days he'd throw it out.

After all, what self-respecting cowboy wore a string of beads around his neck?

Awake by six, Dusty stretched, made coffee and sipped it on the veranda, the clear early-morning air chasing away the cobwebs of sleep.

There, across the yard, Max headed to the stable.

Hard worker. Up late, how late he could only guess, and then up early this morning. No wonder she'd looked so tired yesterday. Had she had coffee or breakfast yet?

He thought of offering to bring her some, but changed his mind. No way did he want to do favors for the prickly porcupine when she'd turned this entire rodeo upside down and had maybe ruined the town's plans to make money.

He had a job to do, dishonest as it might be.

Most knew Dusty Lincoln as an honest guy. This subterfuge didn't sit easy on his shoulders, but the townspeople depended on him.

He sighed and stepped back into the house to dress for his exercises before having breakfast.

From his bag he took out a jump rope to build his thigh muscles, his best defense against re-injury of his knee.

He stepped into the bright sunlight in the yard, hauled his T-shirt over his head and tossed it onto the porch.

He started to skip, slowly at first to warm up, and then faster and faster until sweat rolled down his body, dripping from his face onto his sweat-slick torso.

Morning air cooled his damp back, but the sunshine and exertion kept him warm enough.

He loved exercise and went into another zone, his mind kicking out and leaving his subconscious to come up with solutions to problems in his life.

Unfortunately, not one single solution to the problem of *that* woman came to him.

After feeding the horses and her son's little pony, Max stepped out of the stable…and pulled up short.

The man jumping rope in front of Marvin's house could be none other than Dusty.

As his employer, she should move on.

She didn't ogle her employees, but, cripes, Dusty's body was even prettier than his face, and that was really saying something.

Sweat glistened on every scrap of skin above his sweat-pants. His intimate body parts and his legs were the only bits of him not on show.

The rest shone bare and beautiful.

It had been a long, long time since Max had seen this much of a man's skin bared. She couldn't help but stare.

And then she stared some more.

Her tummy did somersaults.

Her libido, that creature she'd never suspected of existing in her like any normal woman, registered interest in sensitive spots.

Feelings she'd never had before rustled through her like a wandering breeze, like fingers of awareness brushing through soft summer grasses.

Even if he weren't her employee, Max wouldn't know what to do with an experienced man like Dusty. Grimly, she envisioned her amateurish fumbling.

Her cheeks got hot just imagining her embarrassment.

Better to just get on with her day, but she'd enjoyed the show. *Thank you, Dusty, for that.*

She entered the house to have breakfast and move on to the endless chores that needed doing before sitting down to make phone calls to people who probably wouldn't want to hear from her, and who wouldn't want to do what she needed them to do.

An hour later, showered clean, his body humming and his morning hunger satisfied, Dusty sauntered over to the main house.

He and Max had made plans to reach out to contacts to promote the rodeo, Max to the polo players to convince them to participate in Western events and Dusty to every rodeo rider he knew to convince them that, yes, a polo match was a great way to raise money for this town. Or, at the very least, convince them to participate in the other events.

Hard to do when your heart wasn't in it.

He bumped into Marvin and Josh on their way out as he walked in.

"Hey!" the boy said. "Do you like Gramps's house? We bought you groceries. Did you like the lemon meringue pie? That was my idea."

Talkative kid.

"It was real good," he said. "You must be psychic. Lemon meringue is my favorite. I had a slice for dessert last night and another one with my coffee this morning."

The child turned an accusatory eye on his mother, who was resplendent—not—this morning in a wrinkled plaid shirt and jeans that hung loosely on her hips.

A tear in one knee revealed that her freckles went beyond just her face and neck. While torn jeans might be a fashion statement in urban circles, here in Montana it only meant that the faded denim had been worked to death.

She sure didn't put much thought into her appearance.

Had she even combed her hair this morning? It stuck out in spiky clumps, not tame at all.

Dark circles shadowed hazel eyes.

No wonder. As far as he could tell, she hadn't spent many hours in her bed last night.

Her son shouted at her. "You told me I can't have dessert for breakfast ever." He sounded put out as all hell.

Max turned on Dusty with a look that said, "See what you've done?"

Dusty shrugged an apology.

He was a grown-up. He could eat whatever he wanted at any time of day.

Not in the least mollified, Max said, "Adults get to make their own nutritional choices, even if they are poor ones. Until you're Dusty's age, I make them for you."

Thunderclouds formed on the boy's face. Marvin put a hand on his shoulder and steered him toward the door.

"Josh, we got work to do. Let's go." Marvin ushered him outside, effectively cutting off a battle.

Judging by the stubborn look on Max's face, it was a war the boy was never going to win.

"You want a coffee before we get started on those phone calls?" she asked.

Dusty nodded. They headed to a kitchen barely holding its own against encroaching clutter, a stark contrast to the kitchen in Marvin's house.

The living room they passed was a mess, too.

Max wasn't much for housekeeping, but then she had her hands full with ranch work.

Apparently, unlike in his parents' house, Max didn't have a housekeeper.

God, how many balls was the woman juggling?

He couldn't fault her on the mess. Her priorities should be

on making the ranch thrive, but the endless work of ranching life could wear a person down.

She poured them each a mug of coffee. He doctored his with milk. She took hers black, he noted, wondering to himself why that mattered.

They entered a small office near the front of the house, the room he'd seen light shining from last night. So she'd been working in here after everyone else went to bed.

She picked up an account book from the desk, closed it and slotted it onto a bookshelf. Late last night, she'd been either paying bills, or working on finances.

"I'll start with the New York calls," she said, "since it's still so early."

Before they'd separated yesterday evening for their dinners, they'd set the parameters for today's work. They would make the calls on speakerphone and sit in on each other's calls to make certain nothing was forgotten. As well, they never knew what kinds of solutions to problems they might come up with using feedback and complaints from cowboys and polo players.

Max handed him a notebook and a pen.

"If you hear anything useful, or if I forget a good argument, let me know."

Dusty nodded and sipped coffee while she started her calls.

An hour later, he had to give her props. Despite the frustration apparent in the frown on her face and her fingers drumming the desk, she never lost her cool with the men she spoke to.

Her sultry, smooth voice cajoled, argued gently—who knew she even had gentleness in her—and all but pleaded with them to try their hands at Western events.

In Dusty's opinion, some of the men were too flirtatious,

wanting to know if she would date them while they visited Rodeo, but no wonder.

That voice, like sin on buttered toast, hinted at promises Dusty knew she didn't intend to promise or to keep.

Her voice whispered along Dusty's nerve endings. If he closed his eyes, he could forget it was headstrong, argumentative Max and envision a different kind of woman altogether, someone he wanted to get to know better.

Every time a man overtly flirted on the other end of the line, Max made it clear this was strictly business and that it would be smart to keep it that way.

Also every time, she blushed.

This was a woman who didn't flirt, maybe didn't even know how to, and Dusty realized from sitting here watching her how far that voice was from the woman's true character.

Those men were in for a shock when they got here and met her.

None of that mattered as long as she could convince them to cooperate.

Surprisingly, half of them did. It might be enough to make it work.

Even though the polo match video Sam had shown Dusty had been in an amateur league, these were highly fierce men. Maybe once they got here, their competitive juices would kick in and more of them would agree to compete in the Western events.

After the last phone call, Max sat back and tossed her pen onto her writing tablet.

Past frustrated, she said, "Only half of them are ready to commit to barrel racing. Without sufficient training, there's no way they could do anything else, certainly nothing as dangerous as bronc busting."

"True," Dusty said. "But barrel racing's really all they

have to do to entertain the crowd. Even that would be fun to watch."

A grudging smile tickled at Max's lips.

"It would be fun, wouldn't it?" She sobered. "There is one problem. They're afraid of damaging their ponies."

"With good reason. They aren't trained for this kind of thing."

"There must be a way to get around that."

"How about if we ask them to hire Western horses? They aren't worried about spending money on this rodeo. They have plenty. That could be a big win for the community. It would give money to local ranchers."

"Good idea." Max perked up a bit before chewing on her bottom lip. "I don't know what we'll do if the rest don't come around."

Her frown was so deep, Dusty imagined planting hay in the furrows on her forehead.

"Why is this so important to you?" he asked.

"Not just to me, but to everyone on the revival committee. We started this enterprise because the town needs it." She scrubbed her fingers through her hair, mussing it more than it already was.

"We're losing our young people. The next generation is moving away and heading to cities. They can't make money here."

"I see that all over these days."

"I'll bet you do, but we love Rodeo and want to provide jobs here. If we can make this work, we can provide summer jobs for our youth. If it's really a success, we can consider turning it into a permanent fixture that's closed only a couple of months in the winter of each year."

She sat up. "Rodeo is special."

Excitement seeped into her, chasing some of her fatigue

away, making her younger and happier, looking more her own age instead of like a forty-year-old woman.

She couldn't be more than twenty-seven or twenty-eight, at a guess, but she carried the weight of the world on her shoulders.

"The people here are good," she said. "Salt of the earth. Most of them would give you the shirts off their backs."

At the love in her voice, Dusty's soft sucker of a heart responded. The porcupine had a lot of goodwill inside of her.

"We're only halfway through the challenge," Dusty offered. "We need to see if I can convince cowboys to polo. Ride polo. Play polo. However you say it. I'll do my best to help."

Max glanced at her watch and out the window. "I have work to do. I know we agreed that I should sit in on your calls…"

"But you need to get out of here."

"Yeah. Make hay while the sun shines and all of that."

"Okay. Do you trust me to do all I can to convince cowboys to participate in a polo match? What if I try to scuttle the whole thing by convincing them not to come?"

She cocked her head to one side and studied him. He detected not a trace of distrust. "I don't think you would do that."

Right answer. "I wouldn't. You hired me for the job. While you're paying my salary, I'll be honest and do my best to convince the people I know to come." Well, maybe not completely honest. He was here under false pretenses, after all, but while he was trying to sell this polo idea to a bunch of cowboys, he would also try to convince Max to put the bull back into the rodeo.

"Okay. I trust you." She stood and walked to the door. "Bring me up-to-date when you finish, okay?"

"You got it."

She left the room and he got to work.

Two hours later, he wanted to tear out his hair. He cursed Max from here to hell and back. Damn her for asking him to do the impossible. Every single man and woman he talked to outright laughed at the idea.

The town's rodeo would fail, they said.

And Dusty couldn't disagree.

Chapter 4

Dusty had told Max the truth when he'd said he would do the job to the best of his ability, but fighting an uphill battle was the definition of, well, he hated to say stupid, but stupid.

For an intelligent woman, why was she doing this? Why let emotion get in the way of business?

These people involved in the rodeo industry had been blunt in their assessment.

None of the rodeo riders could be swayed into playing polo—not even when Dusty told them that the polo players would be participating in Western events. A few of them wavered for a minute but, ultimately, said no.

Only a couple of hours into the job and Dusty wanted to quit. He wasn't a quitter, and Marvin and the revival committee were depending on him, but he also didn't know what he would do if he couldn't complete the job.

"Hey, whatcha doin'?"

Josh stood in the doorway.

"Making phone calls. It's part of the job I'm doing for your mother."

"What job?"

"To help her organize the rodeo that's taking place at the end of the month."

"I want to do mutton busting, but I don't know how."

"I'm sure your mom could help you, no problem."

"Yeah." The one word came out on a gust of air. "Mom's busy a lot and Gramps has to help her, too. She doesn't have time to show me."

"Hmm." Dusty made sure to keep his tone noncommittal.

It didn't take much to show a kid how to hang on to a sheep, but the way Max raised her child was none of his business.

As far as he could tell from brief observation, the woman worked herself right down to the bone, but where did that leave the kid?

"We got a sheep," Josh said. "Want to meet her? Her name's Doris."

"Doris? That's an old-fashioned name."

"It was my grandma's name. I never met her. Marvin says she was really nice."

Hmm, that didn't sound like the woman Marvin had described last night as Joel's mom, but maybe he was protecting his grandson. "Oh. Well. Your grandma's name. That's nice."

With his thumbs, he rubbed at knot of pain in his temples. Sick to death of the negative phone calls, Dusty stood to take a break.

"Where is Doris?"

"She's out behind the barn."

"I could use some fresh air. Let's go take a look at her. I could show you how to hang on to her."

"I need to ride her, not just hang on. I need to be the best."

Dusty sure understood that sentiment. "I hear ya, kid. I got the same drive to win. Let's go."

They found Doris behind the barn chewing on grass.

Dusty slipped a rope around her neck and led her to a corral beside the stable.

Dusty held the animal still while he instructed Josh. "Okay, this is what you have to do. I doubt Doris will want you on her back. She isn't trained to hold a rider."

Josh sank his fingers into the animal's pelt. "Doris likes me a lot."

"I understand, but it isn't natural for a sheep to have a rider."

"But it's natural for horses?"

"No, but we train them for it. We don't train sheep. Has Doris been trained?"

"No," the boy said. "Okay, I get it."

"So you're going to climb on, but the second you do, she'll resist. All you have to do is to keep the fingers of one hand holding on tightly. Got it?"

"Yep. Let's do it."

Dusty slipped the rope from around the sheep's neck, but held her still while Josh climbed on. She complained immediately.

Dusty grinned. "Told you she wouldn't like it."

A fire lit in the boy's eyes, impressing Dusty. "Let go."

Dusty did and Doris took off. A second later, Josh fell off.

"It's hard," Josh said.

"Sure is."

"Let's do it again." The determined jut of Josh's jaw looked so much like his mother's that Dusty laughed. A chip off the old block.

The second time, Josh rode her for all of two seconds, but hanging off the side of the animal.

"Try to sit upright. Okay?"

"Again," Josh said, with the light of determination in his eyes.

He stayed on a little longer.

Dusty hooted. "Yeah! Way to go."

Josh dusted off his rear end and climbed back on.

Dusty got a real thrill out of instilling excitement about the rodeo into kids. His grin split his face nearly ear to ear.

Every time Josh got right back on the animal, Dusty's excitement grew.

"Yeah!" he shouted.

So did the boy. Josh started to repeat Dusty's yeahs and yeehaws.

Dusty laughed. Mutton busting on a sunny day. What could be better?

They did it over and over, the boy never complaining about the bumps and bruises developing on his butt and knees. Josh managed to stay on better.

"What the *heck* is going on here?" The strident voice startled them.

Dusty spun around. Max stood on the other side of the corral fence with hellfire and brimstone burning up her features.

Max had come out of the stable with a headache forming in her temples.

She'd failed in her phone calls this morning. Only half of the men had agreed to cooperate.

Some might think of that as success—glass half full and all that nonsense—but she needed more than that. She needed the rodeo to be a rousing success.

What if it flopped?

On top of that, she had all her chores to do on the ranch, and she had to drive into town to pick up groceries.

They had enough bread left for grilled cheese sandwiches for lunch, but nothing for dinner.

Her attention was so scattered these days, she seemed to fail in everything she set her hand to. She hated failure. It scorched her gut.

She heard Josh's cute little laugh out behind the stable and it cheered her spirits.

Whatever he was doing sounded like fun.

She climbed into the truck to head into town and turned it on.

Nothing.

She tried again.

Still nothing.

Dammit all to hell and back. Why did everything have to go wrong at the same time? Why was everything so hard?

If she thought the gods, or whoever, would listen, she'd shake her fist at the heavens and give them what for.

She leaned her forehead on the steering wheel, absolutely refusing to give in to a prolonged bout of tears.

Crying wouldn't do her a bit of good, but, boy, did she want to give in. Even more, she wanted to crawl into her bed, pull the covers over her head and sleep for a week.

She'd have to phone one of the local mechanics to make a house call. It would cost her money she didn't have.

She glanced at the house and wondered if Dusty was having any more success with his rodeo friends than she'd had with Sam's rich friends.

Stepping out of the truck, her son's laughter caught her attention again. The adult male voice that responded, Dusty's, and the rousing "yeehaw" had her taking steps around the corner of the stable.

What was he doing playing with Josh when he was here for rodeo planning?

Already burning with frustration, another "yeehaw" had her bounding faster…and there, on Doris, sat her son.

Dusty, the man who should be making phone calls, who should be *working*, stood laughing at Josh's attempts to mutton bust.

Josh fell off and Max gasped.

Dear God, what if Josh hurt himself? He was just a boy— what if something happened to him? He was all she had.

What if he cracked his noggin? Or broke an arm? And how would Max pay for that?

How would she cover the medical bills?

Who would nurse him while she ran the ranch? Who would run the ranch while she nursed him?

The guilt that ate away at her like acid when she depended on Marvin too much to give her son the attention she should be showering on him spurted through her.

Hot and damaging, it felt like shame and, again, failure.

It was all too much. She went off like a rocket on the Fourth of July.

"What the *heck* is going on here?"

Dusty watched Max jump over the fence, easily he noticed, and pick up her son. Big mistake. The boy was getting too old for coddling.

Josh glanced at Dusty and his cheeks turned red. Having once been a kid his age with a doting mother, Dusty understood his embarrassment. He didn't like being manhandled by his mom in front of a man.

"He was enjoying it," Dusty said. He'd never met a woman who could dampen a person's enthusiasm like Max could.

She rounded on him. "I didn't give you permission to teach my son how to ride a sheep."

"No, you didn't, but he wanted to. I didn't think it would cause harm."

"He isn't wearing a helmet."

Dusty leaned back against the fence and shoved his hands into his pockets. "Did you?"

"Did I what?"

"When you were his age and learning mutton busting, did you wear a helmet?"

Her mouth opened. Her mouth closed. "We weren't fully aware of the dangers in those days."

"In other words, no. Neither did I, even though my mother tried to overprotect me, too."

"Over—" Her mouth clamped shut, lips disappearing into a thin line. Only then did Dusty realize how full her lips usually were.

"Get out of this corral right now," she said through clamped teeth. "This isn't part of your job. It isn't what I'm paying you to do."

Dusty straightened away from the fence. Never in his life had he met a more disagreeable woman. "Fine," he said. "I'll head back into the office to do my duties."

"Good."

"You do understand it's usual for employees to be allowed breaks?" He hopped the corral fence while Josh complained to his mom.

"Mo-om, it was fun. I really liked it. We weren't hurting Doris. What's the problem?"

"The problem is that I'm paying Dusty to organize the rodeo, not to teach you how to participate. We have only limited time until that happens."

That didn't ring true to Dusty. This wasn't about the rodeo. Her reaction had been big-time emotional. He strode across the yard.

"That's not the only problem, Mom, and you know it. You don't want me to have any fun." Smart kid.

"Josh, come back here. Josh!"

The boy must have run away. Good for him. Max needed to learn how to let Josh grow.

Inside the office, Dusty threw his cowboy hat onto a chair and huffed out a heavy breath. He hadn't done anything wrong. Didn't even the most junior employee in any company get to take a break?

Cripes, what was her problem?

With an effort he brought himself under control. She had a right to raise her child in any way she wanted, even to coddle him. It was none of his business.

So maybe he should have asked her first if he could show the kid how to rodeo, but he honestly didn't think he'd need to.

Every kid on every ranch learned how to rodeo.

He pulled out his list of rodeo riders to continue the most frustrating phone calls he'd ever made in his life.

"That woman needs to lighten up," he muttered while he put the phone on Speaker, punched in a number, leaned back in the chair and rubbed the tight tendons in his neck. It took only a couple of rings for Chase Coburn to answer his call.

"Hiya."

"Chase, my man, how's it going? Dusty Lincoln here. How're you doing?"

"Been doing okay, 'cept for that win I gave up to you on the weekend. You ready to retire yet?"

Dusty picked up a small rubber stress-relieving ball from the desk, one of those useless gifts people were forever giving to others. At mention of the *R*-word, he squeezed the daylights out of it.

"Yeah, sure," he said. "I'll do that and leave the next bull-riding contest for you to win. Not."

They both laughed. As if Dusty would ever give up a win to anyone.

"Listen, I'm here in Rodeo, Montana." Dusty got to the point. "I'm organizing their revived rodeo. We're pretty excited about it. I want you to come."

Of course Chase would agree to compete—he sounded enthusiastic—until Dusty gave him all of the details, including about the polo match.

"Are you out of your mind?"

Dusty winced. Chase's voice had risen an octave.

"You're not only having a polo match at a rodeo," Chase said, "but you're also canceling the bull riding? Did I get that right?"

It sounded as stupid as Dusty had thought it would.

"Yeah," he said. A frustrated sigh gusted out of him.

"You sound like you don't like the idea any better than I do, Lincoln. So why are you pushing it?"

"It's what the rodeo organizer wants. Not me."

"Okay, you got to tell that guy something from me. No way in hell is any competitor going to come to that rodeo if there's no bull riding."

Chase had a spotless, well-earned reputation on the circuit. The guy could ride. He had a big, bold personality that drew crowds...and Dusty was losing him.

An idea shot through him with the force of one of Cyclone's twirls; the bull was a mean son of a gun with a whole lot of rage inside of him.

Dusty loved to ride him.

"Chase, I agree with you wholeheartedly. Give me a sec to set something up. Don't disconnect, okay?"

Dusty scrambled for his cell phone and set it up to record. "Okay, now tell me everything you just said about pulling bull riding from the rodeo. Feel free to be every bit as colorful as you want to be."

Chase let loose for a good three, four minutes.

Dusty grinned and said, "Thanks, Chase. You've been a big help."

He broke the connection and added Chase's name to the beginning of the recording.

After doing that, Dusty went back and called every cowboy who'd told him earlier that polo at the rodeo would be a losing venture and they needed to add bull riding. He put them all on speakerphone while he asked them if he could record their opinions.

Every one of them agreed to do it.

Once he had a host of negative feedback, he shut off his phone and considered how to present the evidence to his mulish employer.

He sensed Max in the doorway before he heard her.

"I'm sorry," she said. "I might have overreacted." She didn't meet his eye.

"Yeah. You might have." He tried to make eye contact, but she refused to look at him. "I should apologize, too. I guess I should have asked, but I'm not used to so—" he hated to use the word *rigid* when it sounded judgmental "—structured an approach to kids on a ranch."

"You should have, but I guess I understand why you didn't. You wanted to teach him and he wanted to learn."

She tucked her hands into her front pockets and stared at her boots. In her earnestness, she looked downright cute, which was an odd observation to make about Maxine Porter.

"I need you to understand where I'm coming from." She met his eye finally, and he noted vulnerability among the pretty mix of colors. "I loved the rodeo when I used to participate. I love this ranch. I can't imagine another way of life. I love Marvin."

She shifted her weight to the other hip.

"Above all else, I love my little boy. He's really all I have. He's the only blood relative I have left."

Dusty, laden with dozens and dozens of them, couldn't imagine that particular life circumstance, but as much as he needed space from them, he loved every last one of them with all of his heart.

What if he had no one to call his own?

He nodded. "Thanks for telling me that. I understand."

"I do a good job with my son." Her tone had softened and Dusty knew he was seeing a side of her she didn't usually share, all because she wanted him to understand why she protected her son so rigidly. It mattered that she cared about his opinion. He was a stranger, after all.

"He has a good home here and a good life," she continued. "Please don't meddle again. Okay?"

"Okay." Her life was her own. She had nothing to do with him. He was just an employee.

Max looked a little lost, as though she wanted to say more, but didn't know what. She leaned against the doorjamb and picked at a hangnail.

Dusty didn't want the conversation to end, either, which was about as strange as strange got, and he blurted, "Marvin told me about Josh's father. It must have been tough to lose him like that, but—"

She straightened abruptly, probably realizing where he was heading with an argument about the canceled bull riding. Her expression hardened. Touchy subject. "Listen, we aren't going to become friends. You work for me. That's it. No soul baring. No cozy conversations. Your only role here is to make the rodeo work."

She left abruptly, her moment of remorse short-lived.

So much for softening attitudes.

A second later, she appeared in the doorway again. "And don't go talking to Josh about his dad. I take care of those conversations."

Dusty bristled. "As if I would. What kind of guy do you take me for?"

"I don't know. It's hard enough raising a son on my own without having to face down tough questions. Keep your curiosity to yourself. Got it?"

"Yeah, I got it, *boss.*"

She rushed outside, leaving Dusty without a clue as to what had just happened or why.

A friendly guy, he made conversation wherever he went, but making nice with Max was nearly impossible. Fine. He'd keep all his comments to the rodeo. Nothing else.

He thought of Marvin's observations about Max. *She's smart and tough. She's also emotional and sentimental. Worst of all, she's stubborn.*

Max in a nutshell, all right.

At that moment, a tow truck showed up in the yard. Dusty watched through the window while Max talked to the driver, who looked under the hood of her truck and shook his head.

Max slammed her hand on the driver's door.

Uh-oh. Car trouble. A bad thing for a rancher who needed a functioning vehicle.

Not his problem.

He might have more sympathy if she hadn't just taken his head off.

His phone rang. "Single Ladies." He listened as Beyoncé blared.

Mom.

Still angry, he answered with a brusque "Yeah?"

After a moment's silence, his mother said, "That's not how I expect to be spoken to."

A sigh gusted out of him. "Sorry, Mom."

"You don't sound like your normal self. What's going on?"

"It's just this new job. My boss is really tough."

"What's his problem?"

"Her."

"Pardon?"

"What's *her* problem? She's headstrong, that's what. Willful. Highly emotional. Nonsensical."

"You're having trouble with a woman?"

"Why do you sound shocked?"

"I've never heard of your having trouble with a woman."

"I know. It's ridiculous."

"And you can't charm her."

"I'm not trying to charm her."

"You never have to try. You just do."

"Well, this one is immune to my charms." Dusty picked up a pen and balanced the tip on one of his fingers.

"Why?"

"How should I know, Mom?" The pen fell onto the desk with a clatter.

"I can't wrap my head around this, son. Since you were two months old you've had the sweetest temperament. Every woman you've ever met has liked you."

"Not this one."

"Hmm."

"What does that mean? Are you laughing?"

"Maybe. Sorry. I've always thought you had it too easy with women."

"Not this time."

"No, and I find that interesting."

"It's not interesting. It's frustrating."

"Yes, I can hear that."

Dusty hated when his mother sounded reasonable. He wanted her to be indignant on his part.

"She won't do a normal rodeo. She won't let me play with her son. She has rules for everything."

"Rules that you can't charm your way around. She's really shaken you up, hasn't she?"

"I don't like the way this conversation is going. I'm hanging up now."

"Wait!" she said. "What about the picnic on the weekend?"

"I already told you I can't make it. I'll be working. There's a lot to do in very little time."

"Why don't you bring that woman down with you? Bring her son, too. I assume she doesn't have a husband or significant other, or she wouldn't be getting under your skin so much."

"What?" Dusty knocked his empty mug off the desktop. Thank God for the carpet. He bent down to retrieve it.

"Bring her on the weekend," his mom said, sending a surge of horror through Dusty.

"Mom, I'm not coming on the weekend and I sure as heck am not bringing that screwball woman with me."

He disconnected and tossed his phone onto the desk.

A movement in the doorway caught his attention.

Max.

He groaned.

"I came back for my checkbook. This screwball woman is going to have lunch and then get back to work."

She reached past him to retrieve something from a drawer and then turned to leave, but halted. "At six o'clock this evening, I'll expect a report on the phone calls you've made today."

She walked away.

Damn.

Why had he been so honest with his mother? Rather than calling Max names and listing all of her negative qualities, he could have told his mother how much trouble her offbeat ideas for the rodeo were causing him.

Instead, he'd insulted his employer in her own home.

Not smart, Dusty. Not smart at all.

Dusty sat in the blue-gray twilight in his favorite moment of the day, when daytime dissolved into nightfall. An untroubled time of day.

He'd decided to leave the conversation about bull riding, and presenting the evidence of the recorded phone conversations, until the morning when both he and Max were fresh.

Far as he could tell, Max hadn't been having a good day. Piling one more thing on her might have caused the cracks in her composure to give way to an explosion.

He was just as happy to let it go until another day.

Sitting on the front porch, he let the peace of dusk wash

over him, sitting as still and as quiet as a hunter, with his prey being the serenity that often eluded him in his life.

The rodeo circuit was a hectic one in the spring, summer and fall, with extended periods of travel between rodeos.

He endured long stretches of boredom cut with short spurts of the world's toughest, most terrifying and most exciting moments.

Sure, he lived a great life, but sometimes he wanted... He didn't know what. Damned if he could name what that *something* was. Maybe he should—

An argument shattered the stillness.

Sound traveled far when all around lay quiet and still.

Max's husky voice floated from an open doorway, not raised, but firm.

Josh's young squeak of a voice answered. The boy didn't sound the least bit happy.

"But I'm eight years old. Why can't I stay up late to watch the movie?"

"Last time I checked the calendar, today wasn't Saturday. Your late night is Saturday night."

"How come I can only have one late night a week?"

"Because kids flourish best with set routines."

"But I don't *like* my routine."

"Sorry, kid. House rules."

"I hate house rules and I hate you!"

Dusty hissed in a breath. If he'd ever been that mouthy with his mom, his dad would have smacked his backside, miracle baby or not.

"That's unfortunate, honey, but it doesn't change the rules." Max sounded as calm as a granny at a knitting festival. Her son's pronouncement hadn't affected her.

"I'm running away!" Josh shouted.

"Fine. You know where to find me when you're ready to apologize."

"I'm *never* gonna apologize!"

Dusty held his breath, but no response came until a slamming door disturbed the ranch's bats, sending them off in a flurry of black-winged skeletons against the fast-approaching night sky.

A second later, a small figure marched across the yard with a knapsack on his back, trailing a blanket or sleeping bag.

He entered the dark stable. Dusty waited. A light went on inside.

What on earth?

Was the boy going to saddle a horse and steal away? No one followed him from the house to make sure he didn't.

In the short time since Dusty had arrived on the ranch, he'd watched Max with her son. She might not be effusive in her hugs and kisses, but she sure did love that boy.

Her overprotectiveness today proved it, too.

So why was she letting him get away? Why wasn't she overprotecting him now?

A boy that young out on the prairie in the dark, or worse, out on the highway, was sure to get hurt.

Max might not be afraid, but the thought of the boy out alone at night terrified Dusty. God knew where he would end up.

Dusty trudged over to the stable to make sure the child didn't get away, but stopped just inside the door.

Instead of saddling a horse, Josh climbed the ladder to the hayloft.

Dusty listened while the boy rustled around. He heard crinkling paper and then crunching. Was he...? He was eating potato chips.

Minutes later, the lights went out.

There must be a switch up top.

Dusty backed out of the dark stable right into a hard body.

He spun around.

"Sorry." Marvin pitched his voice low, probably so Josh wouldn't hear.

He clutched a rolled sleeping bag under his arm.

"I heard the fight and then saw Josh cross to the stables," Dusty whispered. "I thought maybe he was going to take a horse and leave the ranch. He said he was running away."

Marvin pointed up. "That's as far as he goes. Been doing this since he turned six. At least once a month."

"Is he safe out here alone?" Dusty gestured with his chin toward the sleeping bag. "Is that why you've got that?"

"Yup. Either his mom or I come out to sleep on the old sofa in the office. Tonight it's my turn. We rise early and leave. Josh doesn't know. He thinks he's getting away with something."

Darkness had settled quickly. Dusty sensed more than saw Marvin's grin.

He'd noticed that the older man looked tired. There were ranch hands out and about doing chores in the daytime, but not enough of them. A cost-saving measure, Dusty guessed. Marvin and Max took up a lot of the slack.

"You want to head back into the house and I'll take this shift?" he asked.

"You don't mind?"

"It won't be the first time I've slept in a barn or a stable. Sick horses. Birthing calves. Never a runaway kid, though."

Marvin handed him the sleeping bag. "Have at it. I sleep better in a bed than under a sleeping bag on a lumpy sofa."

"You didn't mention the lumpy sofa."

A soft laugh followed Marvin's retreating back. "Forgot to. Sorry."

The front door of the ranch house closed behind Marvin and all was quiet.

Dusty tiptoed through the stable, barely disturbing the horses. One of them farted, shuffled and settled.

In the office, Dusty found the sofa easily enough, lay down fully clothed and pulled the sleeping bag over him.

Despite the lumps in the sofa, he found comfort in the dry scent of straw and hay, and in the knowledge that this family took care of its own.

He fell asleep.

He startled awake. Something had poked him in the chest.

"Wha—"

"You were snoring," a young voice said out of the darkness.

"Sorry. What time is it?"

"I don't got a watch."

"I don't have a watch," Dusty corrected automatically.

"You do so."

Josh grasped Dusty's wrist and pressed the stem on his watch. The face lit up. Josh skewed himself around, while Dusty tried not to laugh at the child, and said, "I think it's two o'clock in the morning."

"It's the middle of the night. Go back to bed."

"Okay, but you have to quit snoring."

"Aye, aye, boss." Dusty turned onto his side away from the boy, hoping he would take the hint and head back up to bed.

"I gotta go."

"Yeah. Head on back up the ladder."

Dusty heard shuffling behind him.

"I mean I gotta *go*."

"You mean to the bathroom?"

"Yeah. I gotta pee real bad."

"So?"

"So I don't want to go outside by myself."

"You should have thought of that before you decided to sleep in the stable."

"I didn't decide that. I ran away."

Unwilling to quibble over semantics in the middle of the night, Dusty asked, "Where do you usually go when you sleep out here?"

"Nowhere. I always sleep all night, but you woke me up." The accusation in the boy's voice angered Dusty. He wasn't the one who'd run away. He was the one protecting the boy by sleeping on a lumpy sofa. No wonder he'd been snoring.

Josh grabbed his crotch and said, "I really gotta piss."

Dusty's head shot up. "Does your mom let you use that word?"

For a second Josh's jaw tightened with defiance in the weak moonlight seeping through the window before he glanced away. "No," he mumbled.

"Then don't use it. I'll give you a piece of advice, kid, free of charge. Pay attention to your mother. She's the most important person in your life. You've got a good one. She won't steer you wrong."

Dusty sat up and scrubbed the sleep out of his eyes. "What do you want to do?"

"I want to go home. I'm tired of running away. I want my bed."

Dusty sighed and tossed aside the sleeping bag. "Come on. I'll walk you across the yard."

The moon was still new, but the yard and driveway were well-kept and level. It took only a few seconds to cross to the house.

"You okay once you get inside?" Dusty opened the front door. A small lamp glowed on a table in the foyer. Up the stairs traces of dim lighting suggested a nightlight, maybe. Max hoping her son would come home?

"I'm good," Josh said and toed off his cowboy boots.

His bare feet made no sound on the stairs on his way to the second floor.

Dusty stayed and listened until he heard a toilet flush and the patter of feet along a hallway and into a bedroom.

The boy had landed home safely.

Back in the stable, Dusty made sure there weren't any problems in the loft that Josh had vacated, retrieved the sleeping bag from the office and rolled it up. He carried it across the yard, intent on leaving it inside the front door of the ranch house, but a disembodied voice on the veranda halted him.

"Was that you who took care of my son tonight?"

He'd recognize that smoky voice anywhere. Max. Coming out of the darkness, without her boyish garb, it did strange things to his insides. Set them churning and lifting.

She wasn't angry, as she'd been earlier, but soft and grateful, as far as Dusty could tell.

"Yeah. Marvin seemed tired. I told him I'd sleep out in the stable tonight."

"Thank you." The sincerity in her voice warmed him. Silence hung between them, not exactly comfortable, but not awful, either. Why did he find it so hard to talk to this woman? Where was his ease with the fairer sex?

Cripes, if she knew he'd used such a lame phrase, she'd laugh at him. In his experience, women were a hardy bunch.

"Is that Marvin's sleeping bag?"

"Yeah. Here."

When he handed it to her, he brushed her hand, the coolness of her skin a surprise after the throaty warmth of her voice.

She wore a thin nightgown. In the dim light, the palest worn-in shroud covered a body he'd never really got a good look at.

She'd mastered the art of hiding her femininity. Of hiding herself.

Yet again, he wondered why.

"You must be cold," he said.

"A little chilly."

The pauses between them grew long and heavy with expectation. Why didn't he just leave, walk back to Marvin's house and dive into his bed?

Instead, he stood here waiting. Expecting what? He didn't have a clue.

"Well," she said. She cleared her throat. "Thanks for watching over my son."

Dusty had the feeling he'd done more to improve her impression of him by minding Josh than any rodeo win or ranching ability ever could, or even convincing any number of rodeo riders to come to Rodeo for polo.

"Good night." He turned away, the path between the two houses lit just bright enough by the moon to get him there in one piece.

A few yards along, he heard a soft "good night" that trailed him the rest of the way home.

He slept fitfully, the sound of her voice haunting his dreams.

Chapter 5

The following morning, Dusty screwed up his courage to talk to Max.

An easygoing guy, he tended to let a lot of things slide, but this was too important. He'd bet he could put his stubborn backbone up against Max's any day and hold his own. Especially when he was right.

Plus, he thought it wouldn't hurt to take advantage of that little bit of camaraderie or gratitude or détente that had happened in the middle of the night.

He found Max in the kitchen putting the last clean dish into the drainer.

Without preamble, Dusty said, "Can you spare me ten minutes in the office this morning?"

She jumped, put a hand to her chest and spun around. He'd startled her.

"Don't sneak up on a person like that." She scowled at him.

So much for détente.

"Sorry. Can you come now?" The sooner Dusty got this argument over with the better.

She pulled the plug in the sink, wiped out excess suds and followed him to the office.

He gestured for her to sit opposite the desk, while he took the business chair in front of the phone.

"I'm going to get to more of those phone calls in a minute, but first you need to hear something."

After leaving Max on her front porch in the middle of the night, he'd done a lot of thinking. Marvin had said she was smart. Dusty himself had seen her intelligence.

He was betting on her smarts being stronger than her willfulness this morning.

Not a gambling man by nature, though, he took a good long breath before starting in.

"Yesterday I phoned about forty people involved in the rodeo. At first, it was just rodeo riders, but the results were so miserable I branched out to supporters and organizers of other rodeos."

Dusty watched her shoulders tense. She could guess at the coming arguments. She didn't know they wouldn't be his arguments. She already knew what he thought.

"You need to hear this," he said. "These people say everything better than I ever could."

He pulled his cell phone out of his pocket and laid it face up on the desk. She stared at it as though he'd set something dangerous there.

Oh, she could guess what he was up to, all right.

He watched her swallow.

He pressed Play on the recorded comments and an expletive-riddled statement delivered in a loud voice, saying things like, "There's no way in *hell* I'm attending a rodeo that doesn't feature bull riding. Have you gone soft, Lincoln?"

It went on from there, some people more measured in their responses than others, but all agreed that it would never work. The organizing committee in Rodeo, Montana, might as well kiss any chance of success goodbye, each and every person said.

Throughout, Dusty watched Max's face grow pale and he felt sorry for her. Almost.

She'd been living here on her ranch in her isolated little shell not listening to what everyone on her committee and, in fact, the whole town had to say about canceling bull riding.

After the full recording ended a couple of dozen different statements later, from both men and women, riders and organizers, silence settled into the room like a death knell for all of Max's plans.

She swallowed again, rubbed her hands on her thighs and said, "Okay."

Dusty, who'd been leaning back in the desk chair with his hands behind his neck, shot forward.

"What?"

"Okay, add the bull riding back in." She stood to leave the room.

Dusty should have been ecstatic at this major victory, but watching her trudge out, he felt like he'd whipped a small dog.

Only after she stepped out of the house did he grin.

"Yeah!" Good. Now he could get this rodeo organized properly.

But wait. The bull riding was only half of the problem.

He ran out onto the porch.

"Hey!"

Almost to the stable, Max turned.

"What about the polo game?" he called. She'd seen the light. Surely. She had to come to her senses in every area. Right? "It's over. Off the table. We'll have a normal rodeo now."

She shook her head, slowly, and a fierce determination carved her sharp jaw hard. "The polo stays."

"But—"

"It's weird and it will draw a crowd. Mark my words." She pointed to him. "*You* get the bull riding." She jabbed her own chest with her thumb. "*I* get the polo match."

She turned away to enter the outbuilding but tossed back over her shoulder, "Do your job, Dustin. Convince those people to come for the bulls and to stay for the ponies."

The slamming of the door echoed across the yard.

Dusty clenched his fists to stop himself from punching a hole in the wall of the house when he went back inside. Lordy! Lord-y!

The woman made his obstinate mother look like a soft, dewy-eyed saint.

Max could drive a man to drink. He poured himself a coffee.

He cursed long and hard to get it out of his system.

She wanted a polo match? Fine. He'd try to get her a polo match, but most likely he'd end up with a recording exactly like the one she'd just listened to.

But as he entered the office his attitude shifted.

Dusty had never, not once in his life, *tried* to get anything done. He just went out and *got* things done. What was that Yoda saying? Something like "Don't try, only do."

Well, *do* might as well have been his middle name.

He didn't enter into a situation without the only option being success.

Okay, he had the bull riding back in the rodeo. He could offer that to the players. Now he had to throw his heart into getting the polo match up and running.

He started with his best buddy and strongest competitor, Chase, again. As with yesterday, he listened on speakerphone in case recording became necessary.

As he'd expected, Chase cheered about the bull riding, but objected when he heard about the polo. Dusty reminded him that the polo players would be in the same position as the rodeo riders.

"We won't have them involved in the more dangerous events like steer wrestling. There's no way they can compete after only two weeks of practice. We could have them barrel race."

Chase laughed out loud. "You're going to put them in

a predominantly female sport? Now, that would be fun to watch."

"Unfortunately," Dusty said, "we can't have one series of events without the other. Listen, this town needs the money this event could bring in. They're great people. You know how tough it is to keep towns together these days. I know you went through the same thing with your hometown."

"Man, the area was gutted with the number of young people leaving and businesses closing down. It's getting tough to get young ranchers and cowboys to stay home. They love the life, but they need money."

"That's right. Chase, seriously, I'm beginning to think there might be some merit in this unconventional polo idea. What if it's so weird it brings out a crowd just for the curiosity value? I'm drawing a blank here with everyone I'm calling. We need this to succeed to save this town."

"The organizers should have kept to the traditional events."

Dusty leaned back in the office chair. "You know, I thought so, too, but I'm changing my mind. How many rodeos have you been to this summer?"

Chase named a figure. "You should know. You've been to the same events."

"Yeah, and they're popular, but how are we to bring in a larger crowd? What is there to distinguish this rodeo here in Rodeo from all of the others?"

"Nothing unless you do something different. I get your point. But this is big-time different. How are you going to entice rodeo riders who don't currently know a thing about polo?"

"How about appealing to their sense of competition? You know bull riding is testosterone driven. Every man who competes wants to win."

"Yeah, so?"

"So I need to generate that kind of spirit in them for polo.

City slickers versus cowboys is a great way to go. A bunch of city men beating our boys? Come on. That's not going to happen." Dusty didn't mention how tough those city boys had looked playing polo. "I need the word to get out. I need some cowboys to show enthusiasm. I need your help."

"You want me to agree to come and play polo *and* to get everyone else to agree." A statement, not a question.

"That's right."

Dusty didn't interrupt Chase's long silence. He gave the man time to think about his hometown closing down, store by store, family by family.

"You know, those polo horses, so-called *ponies*, look like animals I'd love to take out for a ride."

"You should see what all these rich guys from New York are bringing out. They're worth a fortune and magnificent."

Dusty added one more detail he hoped and prayed he could pull off. "There's a significant purse for the winning team."

He named the figure and Chase whistled. "Even divided among team members, that's a good purse. But, y'know, they have the advantage and are likely to win."

"Yeah, I've thought of that. When I hang up, I'm going to see if I can get those same pony owners to donate the prize to the town if they win."

Dusty held his breath, waiting for Chase to come around.

When Chase finally said, "Okay," Dusty sat up so quickly his belly slammed into the desk.

"Okay?"

"Don't sound so surprised. We need to protect our way of life. If it takes thinking outside of the box, let's do it."

"Chase, I can't thank you enough." Maybe Dusty had inadvertently hit upon the argument that would convince people to participate. He needed to argue that it would help to preserve the Western culture, that big thing that mattered to rodeo riders.

"Don't thank me yet," Chase said. "We both know I'll run into opposition on this."

"They'll listen to you. Everyone respects you, being the second-best bull rider on the circuit."

After a few profanity-laced comments and laughs, Chase hung up.

Dusty studied his list. One rodeo rider down. Only forty or more to go.

He'd hit on a two-pronged approach—everyone's worry about their shrinking towns and way of life, and every rodeo rider's biggest weakness, his love of competition and need to win.

For the entire day, Dusty phoned more of his rodeo buddies and acquaintances.

Each conversation seemed to take longer than the last, as he thought up better and better arguments to use.

When only a couple of them agreed to play, and a few more said they might come on down, Dusty grew tired and frustrated.

To the last man who said he might come, Dusty responded, "Courtney, you know that's not good enough. *Might* is no way to plan and organize an event. I need a commitment."

When Courtney balked, Dusty said, "You're going to hear about this unique event all over the Western states after it's done, and you're gonna be sorry you didn't take advantage of this opportunity to do something different."

Courtney, a young hothead who Dusty had never really warmed to, told him what he could do with his *something different*. Dusty hung up and cursed.

The work was taking its toll.

He scrubbed his nape then stretched to arch his back

away from the bent-forward position he'd maintained for much of the day.

He stared at the ceiling and heard Josh down the hallway. "Can he, Mom? Can he, huh?"

"I don't know, Josh. I have to ask him."

They appeared in the office doorway. Dusty and Max had maintained a wary truce throughout the day, with Max less cool and Dusty more professional and not once saying a cross word about her to his mother when she called today.

"Josh would like you to join us for dinner tonight."

A chance to eat with company would be nice instead of frozen food alone in Marvin's house. Sure, he'd been on the phone in discussions all day, but time spent with real people in conversations instead of arguments would be a welcome change.

"We're having chili," Josh said. As if to sweeten the pot, he added, "Don't worry. There's no beans in it."

Behind his back, Max smiled.

"Oh, well, then, if there's no beans I'll stay for sure."

He followed them into the kitchen. "Is that garlic bread I smell?"

"Yeah, my favorite," Josh said. He gestured toward the kitchen chair beside his. "You sit here."

An informal, hearty dinner followed.

Dusty brought Max up-to-date on everything he'd done that day. He discussed the arguments he'd developed and she approved.

When he mentioned how few men were willing to enter the polo match, only two so far, Marvin and Max exchanged a glance.

"I didn't think you'd get *any*," Marvin said, eyeing Dusty with a puzzled frown, as though to ask, "Whose side are you on?"

On the surface, Max was his employer.

Having been called here on Marvin's behalf, with the committee's secret approval, to kibosh this whole business, getting Max back to offering a traditional rodeo should have been his main goal.

A strange thing happened to Dusty, he'd noticed, while making all those calls.

Ever since he'd seen that video of Sam's, he'd wanted to get up on a polo pony and compete. Aware of the censure pouring from Marvin, he concentrated on his chili, competing loyalties more than he wanted to delve into at the moment.

At heart, a lover, not a fighter, this sneaky role didn't sit well on his shoulders.

"How many on a team?" Marvin asked.

"Only four per side," Max answered. "But we need extra men and horses on board in case of injuries. If we get enough people confirmed, it'd be great to have a round of matches."

Marvin said, "Okay, you've made a start."

Dusty reached for another slice of garlic bread. "I guess I'm used to a more enthusiastic response from these guys than I've been getting."

He did *not* say a word about the bull-riding event. No sense rubbing in his victory.

Max piped up. "I think two is great. Keep up the phone calls tomorrow and see if you can increase that."

She tapped her fingers on the table. He'd noticed tapping was part of her arsenal of nervous habits, including biting her nails.

They were ragged, all right.

"We can always fall back on some locals."

Dusty perked up. "Like who?"

"Michael Moreno. You met him with his children the other day in the diner."

"He must be forty if he's a day."

Marvin stood to clear the table, pressing a hand onto Dusty's shoulder when he tried to stand to help.

"Don't underestimate Moreno," Marvin said. "He's fit. He's quiet, but get him going and he can compete against anyone."

"There's also Travis Read," Max said.

"Who's he?" Dusty accepted the beer Marvin put into his hand. After all of the talking he'd done on the phone all day, it slid down his throat like silk.

"A relative newcomer to town," Max said. "He came just before Christmas, fell in love with Rachel from our revival committee, married her and stayed."

"I need to meet the committee."

"I can arrange it," Max said, adding, "In February, Travis's sister, Samantha, came to town and ended up marrying Michael Moreno. She's our accountant. Anyway, Travis would be willing to help out if need be."

Dusty nodded. "We could use locals and then seed them with any professional rodeo riders who actually show up. Those two men I mentioned are firm. There are a few maybes. In my opinion, maybes don't do us much good."

"I agree." Max stood, maybe reacting to the unusual phenomenon of harmony between them. "It's time for bed, Josh."

The child started to complain, but backed down at his mother's implacable look. Probably didn't feel like running away two nights in a row.

Josh hugged Marvin and kissed his cheek, then did the same with Dusty, stunning him, the small lips on his skin moist and tender.

After Max and Josh left the room, Marvin said, "It fairly takes your breath away with the sweetness, doesn't it?"

Dusty nodded and took a mouthful of beer, swallowing

it hard to disguise the depth of emotion the child's innocent embrace stirred in him.

The second Max's footsteps sounded upstairs, Marvin all but hissed, "What the hell's going on? Why aren't you convincing her to cancel that ridiculous polo match?"

"Y'know, Marvin," Dusty said thoughtfully, "I'm not sure it's such a bad idea. Have you seen Sam's videos of polo matches?"

Marvin shook his head.

"Can you afford an hour to go out to Carson's house sometime this week to watch one or two films?"

"I could probably squeeze it in," Marvin admitted, but grudgingly.

"Do that. Tell me what you think." He stood to leave. "Actually, bring them back here. Ask him for more. I got to study the sport."

Marvin snorted, but promised to do it.

Dusty headed for his own bed and fell asleep quickly, but the frustration of the many conversations he'd had that day put him into an uneasy slumber.

When thunder struck during the night, he rolled over and covered his head with his pillow.

In the morning, Dusty heard a commotion in the yard. As he was about to turn on the coffeepot, he heard Max's mellow voice outside turn strident.

"Get her!"

Huh? Get who?

Josh's high-pitched squeal followed. "I'm *try*ing."

Drawn by the sound of drama, Dusty stepped out into a wet world. Sometime during the night, the heavens had opened up and deposited a good couple of inches of rain.

In the light of day, a half-hearted drizzle still lingered, the clouds having run out of steam by—Dusty checked his watch—eight twenty in the morning.

Rivulets of water ran over ground hard-packed just yesterday, but mucky this morning.

He stepped through puddles of mud, walking toward where Max and Josh chased a cat who made it clear she didn't want to be caught.

"Hey!" Dusty called. "What's going on?"

"Tiger got out of the house this morning," Max said, clearly unhappy. "I need to get her back inside."

"Why? What's the big deal?" He'd never agreed with the concept of indoor cats. Animals were made to live outdoors. Or in barns.

Max stopped running and jammed her hands onto her hips. "She's just had surgery and needs peace and quiet and to be kept clean. I don't want her hit with an infection."

Giving in to the inevitable, because it wasn't in his nature to come across a person in trouble without offering to help, Dusty joined in the chase.

Funny that the cat hadn't already darted so far away it could never be caught. Cats were nimble creatures. Maybe the surgery had slowed her down.

The creature darted between Josh's legs and made a beeline for Dusty.

Dusty caught it. Max lunged at the same time. Her forehead collided with his.

Pain exploded through his head.

His left foot hit a patch of mud and went one way and his right leg the other. The ligaments around his knee stretched past endurance, his knee popped and he went down howling to match the cat's complaint at getting caught.

Max landed beneath him.

Dusty couldn't breathe, the entire world boiled down to the horrendous pain blazing in his knee.

Marvin came running out of the house. Mouth grim, he grabbed the cat from Dusty's arms and carried her inside.

Somehow, Dusty had held on to the creature despite the pain.

He hoped like hell they locked her up for the rest of her natural life.

Dusty rested his aching head on Max's shoulder. Drizzle seeped through the back of his denim shirt.

The backs of his legs were wet.

His knee, white-hot with pain, rested in a puddle.

"Dusty." Max's voice wheezed out of her. "You're heavy."

"Give me a minute." His thigh muscles hurt like a son of a bitch. Unless he missed his guess, he'd not only put his knee out. He'd also pulled a hamstring, a hell of a pair of injuries to have before a rodeo.

Lifting himself onto hands that sank into a mud puddle, he met eyes as riddled with as many colors as he'd ever seen in one person's gaze.

Gold mingled with brown and green and...

Her glare turned to sympathy the second she spotted the pain on his face. Hers reflected pain of her own.

Too bad he couldn't rustle an ounce worth of sympathy for *her*. Anger blazed through him.

He didn't need this. He did *not* need anything that even vaguely resembled an injury at the moment.

He rolled onto his side and breathed heavily, holding in every rank curse and swear word begging to burst out of him in an endless, frustration-riddled howl.

Young Josh watched from a safe distance.

It wouldn't do to educate the boy too early in swearing.

Of all the times to get an injury, just when the knee had healed and he was *that* close to earning another purse in bull riding.

Oh, wait. It wouldn't *be* only bull riding. There would be polo, and he was supposed to compete in all of the other Western events, too.

Now this.

Beside him, Max stirred.

This was all her fault.

He'd come here with the best of intentions, to help these people organize a kick-ass rodeo. Max had hit him with the ridiculous notion of a polo match.

Now she'd hit him with her head, literally, and her stupid cat had gotten out and caused him injury.

He cursed her from here to kingdom come, all with his tongue held firmly behind clenched teeth.

"Are you all right?" she asked.

"No," he ground out.

"What did you hurt?" she asked, rubbing the lump forming on her forehead. "Besides your head."

"Knee," he said. "Hamstring."

Struggling, he managed to stand, but his pants hung like a soggy brown diaper. Max looked as bad as he felt. Mud covered her jeans. Sitting up, she swiped it from her hands and forearms.

Marvin returned and lifted her to her feet.

She stood like a bowlegged cowboy who'd spent a lifetime in the saddle and not much time out of it.

Glancing between them, Marvin asked, "We got any injuries?"

Max touched her head. "I'm going to have a headache later. Dusty, too, no doubt. He pulled a hamstring and did something to his knee."

"*I* didn't do anything," he said, voice thin with agony. "*You* let your stupid cat out."

"I didn't let it out. She slipped out when Josh opened the door to go to the stable this morning. She's crafty and sly."

Josh, looking worried, tugged on his pant leg. "Are you mad at me, Dusty?"

Chock-full of blazing outrage, Dusty couldn't take it out on the kid.

He shook his head and centered all of his anger on Max.

He took one step. His leg crumpled and he groaned. Pain as sharp as a branding iron shot through his knee. Marvin reached to steady him. The man might be getting on, but his muscles were ropy and he was strong.

Dusty tried to take a step to head to his house, but couldn't do it.

"Here, I'll help." Marvin offered him a shoulder to lean on, taking Dusty's arm without a by-your-leave and wrapping it across his shoulder. "That's going to hurt like a b—"

Marvin cut himself off when he realized Josh still stood nearby. "Little pitchers," he mumbled.

The kid's tender sentiments didn't worry Dusty at the moment. His damned leg did. Hamstrings took a while to heal. The real problem was his knee. He'd been trying to avoid turning it into a permanent injury.

He'd wanted to avoid surgery.

Who knew what kind of damage had just been done to it?

With Marvin's help, he hopped to his small house.

"You're getting mud on your clothes," Dusty said.

"Won't be the first time. There's been worse on 'em."

Marvin started to deposit him on the sofa, but Dusty balked. "I need to get out of these pants. The shirt, too."

"You aren't too steady on that leg. You'll need help."

"Help me over to the fireplace."

Marvin left Dusty to lean against the mantel.

"In the dresser in the back room, third drawer down, there's a pair of sweatpants."

"Got it." Marvin left the room.

"Bring me a clean T-shirt, too," Dusty called.

He returned with both.

"Let's get those jeans off you."

Dusty steadied himself on the mantel while Marvin hauled down his jeans. His injuries were bad enough that he couldn't even undress himself. Worse and worse.

"Cripes, I feel like a baby with you undressing me."

"Bet you wished right now I was a woman." Marvin grinned.

"Yeah. Wouldn't mind." Dusty tested the seat of his underwear and found them dry enough. "I can leave these on."

Stripping down out of those would have been too humiliating with everything hanging out while Marvin helped him into his sweatpants.

The man squatted to do just that.

When he'd tied them at the waist, Dusty said, "I can do the shirt myself if you can get me to the sofa."

He sat on the edge, unbuttoned his denim shirt and tossed it on top of his soiled jeans.

Marvin picked them up. "I'll put these to soak in the laundry tub."

"I appreciate it."

After he left, Dusty pulled the clean T-shirt over his head. His leg throbbed. He needed to get ice on the hamstring and his knee as quickly as possible.

Marvin returned and pulled over a small wooden stool. "You think you can put your foot up? Might be best to elevate it."

Dusty tried. "It hurts like hell."

"Hamstrings do, yeah. Knees can be a problem, too. I'll call the doc and get him out here. He'll know what to do."

"So do I. RICE."

"What's that?"

"Rest, ice, compression and elevation."

"We do all of that. We just don't call it that."

"What do you call it?"

"Putting your leg on ice. We got all kinds of stuff here. Max keeps a good first-aid kit."

"It's going to need a lot more than first aid."

"Don't you worry, we'll take care of you."

"How?" Max stood in his living room doorway with a frown worrying her brow. She'd changed to a clean outfit that looked exactly like the last one. She must buy her shirts and pants in multiples.

She bit the nail on one forefinger. "We're busy enough as it is without having to nurse an invalid."

Could the woman be any less gracious?

"This wasn't my fault. I'm an invalid because of your damn cat."

"No one asked you for help."

"Fine." He tried to adjust his leg for comfort. There was none.

"You'll have to stay off that leg for at least a week." She bit the nail on another finger.

"What are you now? A doctor? A nurse?"

"Neither. Nor do I want to be. But I know that kind of injury and how long it takes to heal."

Being a rancher and former rodeo rider herself, she would.

Marvin disappeared from the room, rummaged in the kitchen with something and returned with ice wrapped in a tea towel.

"Sit sideways along the sofa."

Dusty followed Marvin's orders. Marvin lifted Dusty's leg and set the bundle onto the sofa cushion. When he put Dusty's thigh onto it, Dusty flinched from the cold and then settled fully onto it.

Marvin went back to the kitchen and returned with another ice package, which he put on Dusty's knee.

Dusty glanced at his watch to time ten minutes.

Max's frown became more ferocious. "We don't have time for this."

Dusty prepared to blast her for her lack of sensitivity when he got a good look at the worry on her face and realized she didn't blame him. She worried about the whole screwed-up situation when so much work had to be done.

He related to her frustration. It seared through him tenfold. He racked his brain for a solution. "I'll call my mom. She likes nothing better than to fuss."

"Really?" Max sounded dubious. "She'd come out here just because you pulled your hamstring and hurt your knee? Isn't that excessive?"

"My knee is more than just *hurt*. It's damaged." God, he hated that word. He'd spent his young life being as healthy as healthy could be. He didn't like being laid up. "It's an injury that just got made worse than the first time around. We're talking serious *hurt* here."

Sweat beaded on his brow and his upper lip.

"You don't know my mom," he said. "She'll come. You two go on about your business and I'll give her a call."

"How far away is she?"

"A two-hour drive."

"Okay." Max started to back out of the room as though she couldn't wait to put distance between herself and Dusty's problems. "You need anything while you're waiting?"

"Marvin mentioned a first-aid kit. Do you have a compression bandage?" A laugh burst out of him. It was either laugh or cry. "On the other hand, my mom will probably show up with half a dozen of them."

"It'd be best to get one on right away." Marvin left the house, presumably to fetch one.

"What about organizing the rodeo?" Max held one fist inside of the other against her mouth.

Yes, the situation was exactly that screwed up.

"I can make calls from here," he said, his anger abating not the least bit, but they had to move forward. The time constraints worried them both. "I need my notebook from the kitchen table."

She retrieved it for him, passed him his cell phone and left the house so quickly she nearly set up a breeze.

"Mom, it's me," he said when she answered. He knew his voice didn't sound normal and he knew his mom would hear that. "I need you."

"What do you want?" Along with concern, he heard a whole lot of common sense. She wouldn't panic. She'd raised her son to use his noggin. She would know that if it Dusty had hurt himself enough to be in a hospital, he would already be there and someone else would be calling her on his behalf.

He told her what had happened.

"I'll get there in no time. Should I bring your father?"

That would just upset him. Where his mother was practical, his dad would turn into a mother hen if he were to come.

"Nah. Leave him at home to take care of business on the ranch. I'm sorry if this means you have to postpone the picnic."

"Don't you worry about that. See you soon." She hung up. He envisioned her rushing about putting together her own first-aid kit and care package while tossing items into an overnight bag.

On the way, she would stop at a grocery store to stock up, if she didn't remove a few casseroles from her freezer to bring with her.

Marvin showed up at the house with the compression bandage.

"I guess we need to ease these sweats back down."

Marvin helped him do so and wrapped his thigh and

knee. "That'll hold you until the doc gets here. I already called him."

"Thanks, man. I appreciate your help."

"Don't worry about it. Do you want my cell number in case you need anything?"

"I'll take it, but I won't bother you. My mom will be here soon. She'll set speed records."

Marvin left and Dusty settled in to make his next few phone calls to beg cowboys to come to the unlikely polo match in Rodeo.

It was a hard slog, but he gained another two affirmatives, but one was for rodeo events only. No polo.

Even so, it was progress. If he kept at it, maybe they could pull this off, after all.

Without thinking, he changed position on the sofa and hissed on a wave of pain.

And maybe this thing would have to go off without his participation.

The doctor arrived and confirmed what Dusty already knew. He had pulled his hamstring and his loose knee had bumped out and back into position again. The ligaments hurt like hell.

He didn't have any new advice for Dusty. Dusty already knew all that needed to be done.

The doctor prescribed pain medication.

Dusty didn't take the stuff, except when he had to at night to sleep.

He phoned Marvin, who came and got the scrip, then drove to the small pharmacy in town to fill it.

When he returned, Dusty refused to take any right away. He needed his senses clear for the afternoon of work ahead of him.

Marvin left the bottle of pills on the coffee table with a glass of water.

An hour later, Dusty gave in and took a couple.

With pain messing with his thought processes, he couldn't hold viable phone calls. It muddled his mind. He'd just had three people tell him no in a row.

His efforts useless, he closed his eyes and cursed a blue streak.

Chapter 6

"Yoo-hoo. Hello? Anyone here?"

Pleasure suffused Dusty.

His mom had arrived.

"In here," he called.

She entered the house with her arms full of grocery bags. Spotting him in the living room, she stopped. "Dustin Lincoln, what have you done to yourself now?"

"Pulled a hamstring and an injury to the same knee."

His mom would understand the import of that injury, and of how it would be affecting him mentally. He engaged in a dangerous business with the rodeo, with the possibility of injury always present.

She'd tended him a lot of times during his career.

"Thanks for coming, Mom."

She put down her bags, came over and kissed his forehead. "A mother's job is never done. Don't you know that?"

Her hand on his shoulder reminded him of childhood and a world full of goodness. Along with the scent of roses, she brought with her comfort and an easing of his panic.

All would be well.

"Did you buy out the grocery store?"

"Yes, smart aleck. I also picked up a bunch of food from a fab little diner on Main Street."

Dusty perked up. "Summertime Diner? What did you bring me? Vy's lemon meringue pie?"

"Do bears poop in the woods?"

Dusty laughed. Mom could be so corny. It transported him back to childhood.

"I had a lovely conversation with Violet, the diner

owner," Mom went on. "She told me a lot about the town. I like it here."

"Hold on. You drove from home, went grocery shopping, stopped in at the diner, had a conversation with the diner owner and *still* made it here in two hours? Who drove you? Mario Andretti?"

She arched her eyebrows. "I might have sped a little."

"Mo-o-om." He sounded like Josh. "I'm not sick. You didn't have to rush that much."

She patted his cheek. "My son needed me. I'm here. Where's the kitchen?"

"Just shy of the back of the house on the left. You can't miss it."

She left the room, taking her liveliness with her.

"Pie first," Dusty said to her retreating back.

"Lunch first," she called back.

He shrugged and mumbled, "It was worth a try."

Her answering laugh reminded him that he didn't see enough of his parents. In his drive for independence, and to escape his suffocating loving family, he didn't go home often enough.

Through the haze of agony in his leg, he reveled in having a bit of home here in Rodeo.

Max returned from a ride out to check on a sick calf. Mother and son were doing well, thank goodness.

An unfamiliar vehicle sat in front of Marvin's house. Dusty's mother's car, no doubt. She had gotten here quickly.

Honest enough to admit to a certain curiosity about the woman, Max planned to check her out.

She curried Wind and put her away for the day, then walked to Marvin's house. When she knocked on the side of the screen door, a female voice called out from the direction of the kitchen. "Enter."

The woman had a lively voice.

"Mom, it's my house." That came from Dusty in the living room. "At least for the next few weeks. I can speak for myself in my own house."

"Yes, dear, I know, but you're under the weather."

Had there been a hint of…humor in the remark? Max thought so. At Dusty's expense or at the woman's indulgence of him? She got the feeling the woman coddled her son. Why else would she race down here?

Max stepped into the cool hall. Ignoring Dusty, she walked the length of the hallway to the kitchen.

Dusty's mother surprised her. For some reason, she'd expected a little old apple-cheeked woman. Hadn't Dusty mentioned at some point that he'd been a late-life baby? A miracle?

In her late sixties or early seventies, neither in dress nor in attitude did she say *old*.

A trim figure with just a bit of a stomach and hips filled out dark jeans. Her muscled, strong arms, displayed by a sleeveless blouse, might be old, but not flabby. This woman worked hard in her daily life.

Short silver-dusted gray hair framed an unlined face. A soft chin showed the only concessions to age besides a spray of small wrinkles at the outside corners of her eyes and around her lips.

Unless Max missed her guess the woman had taken care of her skin through the years, unlike Max herself, who most days forgot to put on any sort of skin cream, let alone sunscreen.

Violet despaired of her.

Dusty's mother rushed over and wrapped her in a rose-scented hug.

Huh?

"You must be Maxine. I am *so* pleased to meet you. My Dusty has had only good things to say about you."

Considering that Max had heard Dusty's side of one of his phone conversations, his mother had uttered an outright lie.

"He must say those good things when I'm not within hearing range. All I've ever heard is that I'm a screwball and stubborn." She raised her voice enough to make sure Dusty heard her in the other room. She tapped one finger against her lip, pretending to think. "Oh, yes. There was also highly emotional and nonsensical."

She'd also heard him say that she was immune to his charms. Except she wasn't immune. Deep down inside, where she was honest with herself late at night alone in her bed, she admitted that she found him attractive.

He'd turned out to be not all bad, not completely the cocky, self-absorbed man she'd assumed on their first meeting.

In many ways he had his head screwed on right.

She believed he wanted the rodeo and fair to be successful in spite of disagreeing with her plans for it. For that alone, she could forgive him for the many times they'd argued.

Best of all, he'd taken care of Josh that night when her son had run away from home.

"Yes," she repeated, "I've heard him say plenty about me and it wasn't good."

Instead of looking chagrined or embarrassed, Dusty's mother burst out laughing.

"Dusty has his funny opinions, that's for sure."

They both heard Dusty's groan all the way from the living room. "Do you have to talk about me as if I'm not here?"

"Yes!" they both called back at the same time, then stared

at each other with wide eyes. They burst into laughter together.

Max liked this woman. She made fun of herself and she made fun of her son. Max liked her a lot.

"I'm just making lunch," Dusty's mother said. "Will you join us?"

"I'm not sure Dusty would want me to join you."

"Dusty isn't asking," she said firmly. "I am."

So…interesting. Maybe she didn't indulge Dustin as much as Max had assumed.

His mother stuck out her hand. "I'm Charlene Lincoln. Most people call me Charlie."

Max shook her hand, in harmony with another woman whose nickname was that of a man.

"Dusty might have thought he'd been hired by a man," Max said.

"Instead, he was lucky enough to get you." She turned away and stirred something in a pot.

What a nice thing to say.

The kitchen smelled good.

Max's stomach grumbled. "What's for lunch?" she asked, tone wistful. Sick to death of grilled cheese sandwiches on pillow bread, tinned soups and boxed macaroni and cheese, which Marvin and Josh had eaten earlier, her body craved more.

For her son's sake, she should learn to cook, but when? At one in the morning? Her full schedule had plenty of household chores falling through the cracks.

"I'm just throwing together a quick minestrone." Charlie bustled around the kitchen as though she'd lived here forever. Max envied her the ability to be comfortable anywhere. To be comfortable in her own skin.

Each of Max's friends on the revival committee had suffered a lot in life, but they'd come out on the other side confident in themselves.

One by one, Max had watched them find their own definitions of happiness and make it happen in their lives.

All except Max. She lived in the past with judgments about herself made by others that had defined her at too young an age.

She didn't know how to break out of the cycle.

"Not too much of this soup is from scratch, I'm afraid," Charlie said. "I'm using tinned beans and tomatoes."

"You mean sometimes you don't use tinned?"

"Most times I don't, but I need to get food onto the table quickly today."

"Before your son expires from hunger?"

"That's right." She laughed again and Max fell a little bit in love with Dusty's irreverent, fun mother.

A few minutes later, Charlie asked, "Do you have TV trays, by any chance? I'd like to sit here at the table for lunch, but Dustin shouldn't walk or put weight on that leg today. We'll eat out there with him."

"Give me a minute," Max said. "I'll run over to the main house."

Max left, ready to do anything Charlie asked of her. Her own mother had died when she was only ten, leaving Max alone to be raised by her stepfather.

Throughout her teen years she would have walked through fire to have her mother back with her.

She still missed her.

Did Dusty have any idea of his good fortune to have a mother still alive?

"Mom, what are you up to?" Dusty asked, when she came into the room to set him up for lunch with plenty of pillows at his back. "Why did you invite Max to lunch?"

"What do you mean?" Hmm. She might appear to be innocent enough, but he didn't trust her. "She looked hungry. And, to be honest, I think she's lonely. I couldn't not ask her."

"Really?"

"Really."

Well, okay. For a horrifying few minutes, he'd thought she was matchmaking him with Max, a woman so far from his ideal of who he eventually wanted to marry, *years from now*, that he'd recoiled.

But, nah. It couldn't be that.

Max couldn't possibly be anything like the woman his mom would have picked out for him. Mom wore *nail polish*.

On the thin side—he already knew Max put her own needs dead last—Max might appear to a stranger like she needed a good meal. Mom seemed sincere. Maybe Dusty read too much into her intentions.

Lunch turned out to be a lively affair with Mom presiding. Life with her had always been entertaining.

When a kid, Dusty's friends had envied him his great mom. She'd been a decade older than their mothers, but she hadn't behaved that way.

Mom had spent most of her waking hours back then crawling around on the floor with her toddler son. The second Dusty grew old enough for the saddle, though, he'd become his father's child. From sunup until sundown, he spent his days learning mutton busting, roping, riding and just about anything his dad would show him.

A decent rodeo performer in his day, his dad fed every scrap of knowledge he owned to his son, who soaked it up like a miniature cowboy sponge.

To this day, Dusty credited his parents for his successes in life. Yeah, he worked hard, but they had taught him how to do that and love doing it.

He noticed Max watching his mother from across the table, wide-eyed and wondering. It left Dusty trying to understand why. What did Max see when she looked at Charlie? What had her childhood been like? Good? Bad? What had happened to her parents?

He would have to ask. But no. Why would he? He'd be here for only three more weeks. After he finished the job, he'd head on out to his next adventure with Maxine Porter nothing more than a footnote in his life.

"Mom?" The small voice from the other side of the screen door was Josh's. "Are you over here visiting Dusty? Who belongs to that strange car?"

"C'mon in," Dusty called before his mother could make free with his living space again.

Josh entered and his mother went into raptures. *"Who is this?"*

"My son, Josh," Max said and damned if she didn't look both shy and pleased, proud as punch to be able to share the mothering experience with *his* mother.

"Have you had your lunch?" Charlie asked Josh, because above all things she liked to feed little boys.

"Marvin gave me macaroni."

"Marvin?" Charlie asked.

Mom knew Marvin darned well, but put on a good show to hide Dusty's secret.

"He's my grandpa," Josh said.

"Would you like to try some minestrone soup?" Charlie jumped up to get him a bowl, but Max stopped her.

"Let him try mine first." Max drew him near. "It's good. Try macaroni cooked like this."

Josh ate a piece of elbow pasta. "I like it." He sounded excited. "Are those beans?" He sounded skeptical.

He tried one and wrinkled his nose.

"Oh, come on," Max said. "You like toast and beans. A bean is a bean is a bean."

"Have a bowl of soup," Charlie said. "And what about your grandfather? Would he like some?"

Max whipped out her phone and called for Marvin to come over.

A second later, he knocked on the door. Minutes later, he came under Charlie's spell along with Max and Josh.

Oh, Mom. I do love you.

At one o'clock, Max and Marvin left to do chores, taking Josh with them.

He asked to stay, but Max told him Dusty had to rest. "Either that, or make phone calls."

"Yes, boss."

Minutes later, a knock on the door accompanied giggles.

Charlie opened the door and led a bevy of beauties into the living room. Dusty recognized the two young twenty-somethings he'd met in the diner on his first day in Rodeo.

It seemed they'd brought friends with them to visit.

"We heard you got hurt," one of them said.

No dust gathered on Rodeo's grapevine. These young women must have set in motion whirlwinds getting dressed up and putting on heavy makeup, showing up here tottering on high heels like they headed out to a club for the night.

They were all beautiful in their individual ways, but every one of them had overdressed for an afternoon visit to a ranch.

Not in the mood for flirtation when he'd come to town to work, with time limited and his brain fogged with pain, Dusty wondered how to get rid of them.

Charlie opened her mouth to offer hospitality, but Dusty stopped her with a shallow shake of his head.

He didn't want them staying long.

She left the room. He heard her in the kitchen cleaning the lunch dishes.

The women took seats around the room without being asked.

One of the bolder of them actually sat on the end of the sofa. When it dipped, and his leg followed suit, he hissed.

"Oh, you're in pain!"

"We should do something."

"What do you need?"

Once upon a time Dusty would have reveled in the attention, but at the moment it left him cold. His age catching up to him, maybe.

Or maybe he liked more interesting conversation.

Or maybe he wanted to get back on his phone and persuade more rodeo riders to come here and play polo.

He missed something one of the women said.

"Pardon?"

"I asked if you want to come out to Honey's Place on Friday night. There's always a great band on the weekend."

The local watering hole, he assumed.

"I won't be able to dance," he said.

"Won't your leg be better by then?"

"I'll be lucky to be walking by this time next week, let alone dancing this Friday night."

He recognized the look in her eyes, interest in him that bordered on avidity.

The girls conversed among themselves while Dusty got more and more tired. He studied the women and listened to them talk and understood exactly what they saw in him.

A way out of small-town Montana.

Each and every one of them viewed him as their ticket out of Rodeo. Each thought the particular highway they needed to ride out on looked like him, that if they hooked up with him he would show them the world.

He raged against that mind-set.

For an easygoing guy, he had a strong urge to scold them, to advise them to find out who they were in their cores, to decide what they wanted in life and go after it. He thought one or two of them would understand. The others just wanted an easy way out. Maybe he should give these women more credit, but experience had taught him this. Achievement tasted sweeter when attained on one's own merits rather than hanging on to someone else's coattails.

He glanced out the window.

Max rode into the yard on one of her horses and dismounted in front of the stable. Now, *there* was a woman who worked hard for everything she had.

Dusty might not like her, but he respected how well she dealt with her responsibilities. She might worry, but she didn't complain. She put her head down and got the work done.

Despite this morning's setback—he grimaced thinking about it—she'd worked on the ranch all morning and again right after lunch. He wondered if her head pounded from when they'd collided earlier.

The way she'd felt under him… Even riddled with pain, he remembered how it felt to sink into her for support, as if his body knew how right it felt, even if his head didn't want to.

Slow down, Dusty. What does that mean?

But something puzzled him…something that felt off. Now that his thoughts had a chance to wander, he realized his mind had registered more about her than he had thought at the time.

As much as she tried to hide herself behind loose shirts and baggy jeans, a man's touch told him a lot.

His chest had felt those unnaturally flat, hard breasts

and a corner of his mind had stored that detail away for future thought.

He shook his head. How could he have sensed something wrong about the way they felt?

Well, duh. He'd been with enough women to know how a woman's different parts should feel. His eyes swept the room as the women continued to chat. Case in point—he'd never had trouble finding female company.

What did Max hide?

Or was she hiding anything?

He glanced back out the window to find her staring at the two cars the women had arrived in, parked in front of Marvin's house.

Dusty could practically see the wheels spinning in her brain, no doubt blaming him for not getting his work done.

Unless he missed his guess, he'd be hearing about her displeasure at some point.

He leaned back against the cushion and crossed his hands behind his head, gearing up for battle.

Bring it on.

It struck him that a part of him liked seeing her all fired up with passion in her eyes. He grinned.

Unfortunately, he happened to be facing the woman almost sitting on his leg. She mistook his inner musings for attraction.

Damn.

He schooled his expression to neutrality.

Over the years he'd monitored his reactions so he attracted only the girls he wanted and didn't hurt others.

He sounded full of himself.

Sometimes he wanted to shout, "I'm nothing special. I'm just an ordinary guy."

He loved female attention, but right now, with his leg

pounding a percussive tune and his temples threatening to join the band, he wanted rest.

Mom peeked her head around the door from the hallway, raising her eyebrows.

Dusty scrubbed his hand through his hair. She nodded. They'd set up that signal years ago. Dusty hadn't used it in a long time—not since his teen years, when girls used to visit the ranch and hang around, and all Dusty wanted was to ride or practice roping.

Tired, and needing to return to important rodeo matters, having his mom around to run interference, even at thirty-one, worked.

She entered the room and said briskly, "It's time to leave, ladies. Dusty needs to ice his leg and I need to change his bandages."

Change bandages? What bandages? Not one of the women had asked him about his injuries. They would have no idea his mother lied.

They scooted out, but not before making sure to give him all kinds of invitations to come visit them.

Max timed them.

Despite all of the work waiting for her, she'd wasted a bunch of time watching Marvin's house to gauge how long the women stayed.

As her employee, Dusty should be working.

Because of his leg, she'd decided he could nap if he had to. Instead, the man sat inside entertaining half a dozen young women.

When the two cars drove off, she stomped across the yard, onto Marvin's porch and into the house.

"I told you to either work or nap." She sailed into the living room with both barrels blasting.

"For the love of God," Dusty snapped. "They came here

without an invitation. What was I supposed to do? Kick them out? Refuse to see them? I'm not rude like *some* people I could mention."

Max didn't understand the gleam in Dusty's eyes. Did he…did he enjoy fighting with her?

Charlie appeared beside her, wrapped an arm around Max's waist and steered her out of the house, ever the protective mother hen.

Max wanted a mother hen of her own.

Charlie tossed over her shoulder, "Rest, Dusty."

She maneuvered Max toward the stable. "Show me your horses."

"Okay," Max said meekly; an older woman touching her in a motherly way felt heavenly. In fact, it felt so good it made Max weak and a little weepy.

"Dusty's always been a charmer where the ladies are concerned, but he has a kind heart," Charlie said. "I watched for a while with those girls who were visiting, and then I rescued him. He can't stand to hurt women's feelings."

Max snorted. "He never worries about hurting *my* feelings."

"Yes." Charlie sounded thoughtful. "I noticed that."

Charlie admired every horse Max owned. She also admired Josh's pony when he joined them.

She asked intelligent questions about the ranch.

Max hadn't talked to a woman about ranching in so long that she reveled in it.

Only later did she realize how Charlie had mollified her about the young women visiting Dusty…and somehow she didn't mind being manipulated by the woman.

Chapter 7

Dusty awoke to the scent of bacon frying in a skillet and the sound of his mother singing in the kitchen.

An answering female voice disturbed him. Haunting, like from a dream. Husky hints of vanilla tickled his nerves.

Hints of vanilla? Tickled his nerves?

He must have hit his head harder yesterday than he'd first thought. Something had cracked.

Or maybe he just needed breakfast.

Leaning against the coffee table, a pair of crutches awaited his use.

Max, or maybe Marvin, must have left them here. Good. He needed them. He couldn't lie around all day. It went against his nature to be idle.

Gingerly, he sat up and grasped the crutches. He hauled himself to his feet and hobbled without grace to the kitchen.

Two women, one young and one older, sang in perfect harmony to "Single Ladies."

Dear Lord, he'd landed in hell. No to rings. No to commitment.

A lot of carefree years awaited his future.

He stood in the kitchen doorway.

His elderly mother's jeans fit her better than the baggy ones hanging from Max's butt. He'd tossed and turned last night with the pain from his injuries, and had finally fallen asleep thinking about yesterday's revelations about her. What *was* Max hiding? And why?

The women he knew had no trouble wearing clothes that fit. He'd known plenty who flaunted their bodies with tight clothes and low necklines. He just liked a woman to dress to suit who she was or wanted to be.

A small voice of reason argued, *Maybe Max is dressing to suit who she wants to be.*

Yeah. Could be. But why did she want to be shapeless?

"Did you bring these?" he asked, his voice morning rough and starved for coffee. He held up one crutch.

Max spun around. The smile she shared with his mother disappeared…and his gaze dropped to her chest.

She cleared her throat.

He brought his eyes up to her face. *Cripes, Dustin. Get a grip.*

He loved women, but he didn't walk around staring at their breasts.

He gestured with a crutch. "Were these your doing?"

She nodded. "Marvin sprained his ankle last year."

"Thanks." Of his mom he asked, "What's for breakfast?"

"Good morning to you, too, sweetie." She approached, kissed his cheek and patted his shoulder. "Love you."

He grinned. "Sorry. I'm surly this morning. Love you, too."

Max's eyebrows shot up. Why?

A small voice piped up. "You said 'love you.' Boys don't say yucky stuff like that."

Josh sat at the table finishing up a plate of pancakes.

"Boys say 'love you' to their mothers all the time any-time," Dustin said. "They like it a lot when you do that. That's a good lesson to learn, kid."

"Right answer, Dusty." His mother handed him a coffee and bestowed on him her proud-of-you smile.

Warmed through, he sipped the coffee, set it on the table and headed to the washroom, awkward on the crutches.

Back in the kitchen, he sat down to pancakes and sausages.

"Josh, are you over here?" Marvin's voice rang through the front screen door.

"C'mon in," Dusty called. "Might as well. Everyone else is here."

Once Marvin entered, the small kitchen felt crowded. Strangely, Dusty didn't mind. Often in his parents' kitchen, relatives packed in at any time of day or night.

He'd come to resent the lack of privacy.

Now that he lived on his own, moving from place to place, weekend after weekend, today's camaraderie warmed his cozy kitchen.

Marvin declined a coffee. "Thanks, but there's work to be done."

The older man took Josh away for a ride to check on cattle and then there were three.

Dusty's happiness turned to discomfort, with all of his self-discipline strained by training his eyes on Max's face instead of her bust. Her chest area shouldn't matter to him.

As though she sensed his tension, Max's shoulders squared.

The two of them tended to circle each other like a pair of wary tomcats. This lack of skill in dealing with a woman upset him.

Max nibbled on a nail. "Will you be able to work?"

He stiffened. "I can still handle a phone, just like I did yesterday."

"But there's legwork involved in putting a rodeo together. Literally."

Dusty shot her a look. "Don't blame me for this injury. You're welcome for catching your cat, by the way." His mother stared at Dusty's uncharacteristic sarcasm.

Max cocked an eyebrow. "Well, don't blame me, either."

"I'm not!"

"Don't yell at me."

"I don't yell!" he yelled. "Ever."

Max pursed her lips, and for the second time he noticed how full they were. The woman ruffled him so much—he had the sudden urge to lean over and kiss that sour look off her face.

What the hell?

"Cut it out," Dusty's mother chimed in, sounding good-natured but firm. And not a moment too soon—what was with him today? "I'm certain the two of you, being adults and not children, can work this out. This injury is merely a wrinkle. It isn't the end of the world."

"You're right. We'll get through this." Dusty's taut shoulders eased. Max's didn't.

"Thank you for breakfast, Charlie." She left the room without saying goodbye to Dusty.

"Well," Mom said. "Well, well."

"Never you mind with your *wells*." Dusty sounded ungracious and he didn't care. He didn't like not understanding a woman and especially not understanding his reaction to one. "You got any of that lemon meringue pie left? It's good with coffee."

Max shouldn't be hurt. She wasn't. She sure as hell was not.

Even so, why could the guy be nice to everyone else but not to her?

Marvin and Josh led their horses out of the stable, Josh's pony almost too small for him. One day soon she was going to have to buy him a horse. But the money...

Marvin approached. "Why do you look angry? What bee crawled up your butt this morning?"

"I need to buy Josh a real horse."

"He's good for a while yet." He helped Josh to mount and her son trotted out of the yard.

After making certain Josh passed hearing range, Marvin asked, "What's really bothering you?"

Marvin had become a dear friend over the years.

What would she have done without him taking her in all those years ago, when she was terrified and alone? She'd worked hard for him, even while pregnant, until she'd bought the ranch from him, and had become the owner and he the employee.

The women of the rodeo and fair revival committee might be her confidantes, but Marvin had been here on the ranch with her day in and day out through thick and thin. He was the closest thing she had to a father, after losing hers as a child.

"Spill, Max." Marvin's horse stirred restively. He controlled the big animal easily.

She tapped her fingers against her thigh. "Why would Dusty be nice and charming with all the other women on this earth but not with me?"

"How do you know he is?"

"Charlie told me, yesterday in the stables." She muttered, "After he'd entertained half of Rodeo's female population."

Marvin bit his lip.

"Are you smiling?" she asked.

"No."

"You wouldn't want to do that at my expense, right?"

"Course not."

"Good. I'm glad we got that settled."

"Take a hard look at how you treat Dusty," Marvin said, returning to Max's original concern.

"I treat him just fine." If she sounded strident it only made sense. The question made her defensive. She'd treated the man well at first. It had been Dusty who'd gotten her dander up.

Or had it?

"When you brought him home that first day from town, your back was already up."

Marvin had a point.

"Why?" he asked. "What had he done or said to you?"

Marvin's incisive stare unnerved her, making it impossible to fudge the truth, let alone outright lie.

"Nothing," she admitted.

"Then what was your problem with him?"

"The women were all over him."

"What women?" Marvin's horse nudged his shoulder to get him to mount up and ride. Marvin ignored him. "Where'd you meet? In the diner?"

She nodded. "You should have seen the women falling all over themselves to get his attention. Asking for his autograph. I need a man to take this job seriously and get this rodeo off the ground."

"Hasn't Dusty been working hard at that?"

"I guess."

"Max, be honest," Marvin admonished.

"Okay, yes. He's a hard worker."

"So it isn't his work ethic that's bothering you." He mounted to ride out after Josh. "As soon as you figure out the rest, come back for another talk."

He rode off, leaving Max to ponder what the *rest* meant.

The following morning, Charlie entered the living room with a worried frown. She set a cup of coffee down at Dusty's elbow.

"What's up, Mom?" Dusty asked. His stomach tightened. He'd heard her phone chime a few minutes ago. "Is there something wrong with Dad?"

"No, no," she soothed but still looked worried. "It's your aunt Marcie."

"What about her? Is she hurt?"

"No. It's her daughter. Belinda's been admitted to the hospital with preeclampsia."

"Pre-what?"

"It's a condition pregnant women get. It's high blood pressure and dangerous for both mother and fetus." She waved her hands in front of her. Weird. Mom was unflappable, yet here she was flapping.

"You know Marcie," she said, "and how she worries about Belinda. She's such a worrywart."

Mom's younger sister was as rock-solid as Mom was. She didn't flap. She didn't worry. She'd raised Belinda to be confident and full of backbone.

"What are you up to, Mom?"

"Up to? Nothing. I have to go."

"Go?"

"Yes. I'm driving home to offer my support to the sister who needs it desperately."

Dusty burst out laughing.

Mom glared, indignation written across her face. "Belinda's condition is not funny."

"No, but you are. You've got to be, hands down, the world's worst actor." He shifted on the sofa. His hamstring might be protesting a little less today. Marginally. His knee still hurt like a son of a gun. "Cut the crap, Mom, and tell me the truth."

"Fine." She sank into an armchair and smiled, back to her usual self. "I'm driving home this morning."

Dusty pointed to his leg. "And this?"

"You'll have to find another nurse."

"Why?"

"Because."

"Because why?"

She studied him.

"Come on, Mom, you can't fool me. Tell me whatever scheme it is that you've hatched."

She gave in with a delicate shrug. "Might as well tell you the truth. It's Max."

"What about her?"

"I can't for the life of me figure out what she has against you."

"Don't look at me for answers. I can't figure her out, either." Dusty took a sip of coffee. His mom brewed a better cup than anyone he knew.

"I think if she has a chance to spend time with you she'll see what a wonderful person you truly are."

Dusty choked on the coffee he'd been about to swallow. "Spend time? How?"

"I think she should be your nurse."

"My *nurse*? There isn't a woman on this earth less suited to nursing and nurturing."

"Now, there you are wrong, son. Have you seen her with Josh?"

He had. She did well by him and gave him plenty of affection.

"She's not warm and cuddly, Mom."

"She doesn't have to be cuddly, only competent. How hard is it to check on you once in a while?"

"Mom, this isn't like you. You've never abandoned me in the past."

"I'm not abandoning you, but Max and you have to come to terms with each other. She is your boss. You are her employee. I've never seen you behave unprofessionally before."

She knew him well. He'd learned professionalism early on in the competitive world of rodeo.

He'd let his standards slip with Max. He shouldn't be arguing with her. He shouldn't be thinking about kissing her.

"You have to work together if you are going to make the

rodeo a success." Charlie stood. "Violet told me how important the success of this venture is to the town. Try to get along with Max. I know you can, Dusty."

He knew that look, the one that said she wouldn't be swayed from the course she had set no matter what.

"Okay."

"Thank you, honey." She hesitated and he waited.

"Do you think," she said, "what you and Marvin are doing is right?"

Dusty shifted uneasily. A tough cookie, Max would be okay. Besides, she would never find out, would she?

"Isn't it unfair," his mom went on, "to fool a person like this?"

Dusty didn't know how to respond. He'd never done anything this dishonest before.

"Tell her why you're here," Charlie urged. "Tell her that you know Marvin."

He shook his head.

She raised her hands and then let them drop into her lap. "At first when your dad explained why you were here, I thought it was a good idea, for the sake of the rodeo. Since meeting Max, I have serious doubts."

"Me, too," Dusty admitted. "But I don't know how to change it now. Anything I say will hurt her. She'll feel like Marvin betrayed her. I've got to just help her to make the rodeo as successful as this town needs it to be and then leave. She'll never know."

"Are you sure that's the best way to handle it?"

"Positive, Mom." Now that he knew Max he didn't want to wrestle with her about his deceit. Best to get through this ordeal unscathed.

Charlie's expression admitted defeat. "I did my best. I have to pack. Tell Marvin I washed his bedsheets and remade his bed."

She made for the door but Dusty stopped her. "Wait, are you honestly torn up about this?"

She sighed. "No, you have to handle this how you see fit, but…" She paused, as if weighing what to say.

"But what?"

She sat back down. "Well, I might as well just come out with it. You're going about this all wrong. I only say that because I like Max." Her gaze met his directly. "I like her for you."

Her meaning dawned on him, as did mounting horror. "Mom…just what the heck are you talking about?" Dusty all but shouted.

She huffed out a breath. "Okay. So let's see. I want you to be happy. I want you to be in love and to love and to be loved. I want grandchildren. That just about covers everything."

Grandchildren! Love! Where had this come from? "You're jumping way ahead of reality," he said when he could speak.

"Yes, I am, but with good reason. I'll be the first to admit that you, as my wonderful miracle baby, were indulged as a child. Somehow, you turned out to be a fine young man. Incredibly sweet."

Sweet? He thought of himself as sexy. Rough and tumble.

"You aren't spoiled in the traditional bratty sense," she continued.

"Thanks, Mom," he said drily. "Why do I sense a *but*?"

"Because there is one. Plenty of good things in life, and especially women, have come to you easily. Max is one woman you can't charm."

Dusty shrugged. "So?"

"So, you've met your match, son. I always knew you would. She doesn't want the charming boy you've always been. She wants a man who lives a lot more deeply than you do."

He scowled. "What's that supposed to mean?"

"It means that a relationship with Max won't come easily. She could be the making of you as a man."

Dusty resented his mom's characterization of him. He didn't need Max to *make* him. "Max and I don't even like each other, let alone are in danger of falling in love, but you've got us getting married and having babies."

"That's right."

He shook his head, so damned bewildered. "I barely know the woman."

"Considering that you hardly know her, you sure have a strong reaction to her. I find that interesting."

"It's not interesting," he shot back. "It's nothing. Okay? It's not a reaction *to*. It's a reaction *against*. There's a difference."

Charlie crossed her arms at her waist. Rarely militant, his mom sure looked it now. "Explain the difference to me."

He didn't know the answer. "Let me put it this way. I don't find her attractive."

"Because of the way she dresses?"

"Maybe. I don't think so. You know that kind of stuff doesn't carry weight with me. I like what's inside. A lot."

"True. I do know that about you. But if the problem isn't the way she dresses, what is it?"

"She's too— Mom, I think there's something wrong."

"What do you mean? Wrong how?"

He shrugged. "I think there's some serious stuff going on inside of her that makes her hide herself. The only person I ever see her really let down her guard with is Marvin. The only one I see her really show love to is her son."

"She might just be an introvert."

"Probably, yeah, but I get the sense that she's damaged. Or there's been some damage done to her."

"Can't you deal with it?"

"I don't know if I want to. I mean, I have a good life. I'm having fun. Why would I want baggage?"

"Good question. Figure it out and call me."

"No. I mean I don't want it. I don't want to take it on when there are so many uncomplicated women out there."

"True, but uncomplicated women might not be as interesting."

Dusty thought his mother's arguments through.

"Let me ask you something."

"Go ahead," she said.

"You barely know her. She's hard-edged and stern. She has no sense of humor that I've seen. What on earth do you like about her?"

"Her very sweet vulnerability."

"She's not vulnerable."

"She is."

"I haven't seen any trace of that."

"You certainly have. You always were a sensitive little boy. You've grown into a sensitive man, when you want to be and you're not too busy having fun. You've already guessed that she's damaged. Ergo, you've sensed that she's vulnerable."

"I haven't seen any such thing," he insisted.

"No? Look deeper, son."

She left the room and returned a moment later with her overnight bag.

She kissed his cheek, said, "Love you with all my heart," and left the house.

Dusty picked up his empty coffee cup to throw across the room, but thought better of wrecking Marvin's place.

He set it down on the side table with an audible *clunk* and pounded the side of his fist on the arm of the sofa, absolutely refusing to play his mother's game.

* * *

Max saw Charlie put her overnight bag into her car.

A frisson that felt very much like panic ran along Max's nerves.

She didn't want Charlie to go. She liked her and liked having her on the ranch, just so Max could walk over for a hug.

How needy was that?

She didn't even know the woman. Not really. Charlie had only been here a couple days and yet…

The thought of her leaving left Max bereft and a little teary-eyed.

She needed— Oh, God, she didn't know what she needed.

Charlie walked toward her and enveloped her in her arms.

Max sighed.

This was what she needed. How did the woman know?

She blinked to clear her blurred vision, so damned tired of doing it all alone. Of always holding herself together when she wanted to cry.

She loved Marvin. He'd been a rock, but sometimes she wanted someone else to take over for a while, to paddle the unstable tippy canoe of her life across choppy waves to a serene shore, just for a few minutes. Or more. For a few days.

Never in her life had she had a holiday. She couldn't remember the last time she'd taken off for the weekend. When had she last had a full day off?

Charlie smelled like a bouquet of roses, old-fashioned and totally, beautifully nice.

Dusty's mother didn't let go. Apparently, Max had to do that when she'd had enough.

She never would but forced herself to ease away from Charlie.

"You're leaving?" Her voice hitched. She hoped Charlie hadn't heard.

"Yes."

Charlie explained why, but in her sorrow at losing this treasure she'd only just met, Max missed most of it. Something about a niece and a high-risk pregnancy.

"Come visit me sometime at my ranch," Charlie said. "Okay? Promise me?"

"I would love to, but I can never get away."

"You'll make a point of it," Charlie ordered. "I can't come back until next week so you're going to have to take care of my Dustin."

"Oh, but—"

Charlie patted her cheek. "Thank you, sweetie. I trust you to do a good job."

"I couldn't possibly—"

"I know he can be a handful. You'll never know how much I appreciate this." She got into her car and drove off with a cheery wave through her window.

"But..." Max's whisper trailed off into thin air.

"Welcome to my world."

Max spun around.

Dusty leaned on his crutches on Marvin's small porch, judging by his disgruntled expression, none too pleased with this new turn of events.

Well, neither was Max.

"My mom is a force to be reckoned with."

Max couldn't agree more, but she liked her. Adored her. Dust kicked up by Charlie's car drifted to the ground, the rain of two days ago already dried up in the unrelenting summer sun.

She turned back to stare up at Dusty.

"I'm a terrible nurse," she said.

"I'm a worse patient."

They stared at each other in some kind of weird stalemate, both loving and resenting Charlie for what she'd done to them.

A smile kicked up a corner of Dusty's mouth, an acknowledgment that he understood everything going through Max's mind.

Max's traitorous heart stuttered when that shadow of a dimple made an appearance. A thatch of messy blond hair, deep blue eyes, white teeth and also a dimple.

No wonder women fell all over him.

Not her. Immune, she stiffened her resistance. She liked real men who stuck around and worked hard. She liked more from her men than—

That thought had her laughing. *Her men?* What men? There weren't any. There had only ever been one, Joshua's father, and their relationship had been brief.

A one-night love affair.

No way would she share that unfortunate pity-inducing detail with a man like Dusty. He could have any woman he wanted…and probably had.

"We're quite the pair," he said. "Terrible and worse. Between the two of us we'll get by."

He leaned on his crutches heavily and turned to hobble back into the house, pain making his lips white around the edges.

Not so happy and carefree, after all.

Max could almost feel sorry for him, until her sense of duty kicked in.

"I'll be back later," she said. If she sounded like she resented having to do so, well, who could blame her?

She dealt with a full plate every day.

"Mom, ow!" Josh's voice, sharp and in distress, caught her attention.

She whipped around, her mother's instincts on high alert.

Josh ran toward her on the brink of tears holding out his hand.

"Look." He shoved a blood-tinged thumb at her.

Her heart switched from fear to tenderness, melted by his little-boy misery, the fear appeased by the triviality of the injury. "Oh, hey, what did you do?"

"I cut it."

With a hand on the back of his neck, she steered him toward the main house.

"Bring him in here," Dusty said. "It's closer."

She followed him into Marvin's hallway, slowed by his halting progress.

"Let's see what you did, Josh," Dusty said, easing himself onto the old couch. "Sit here."

Josh did, showing off his thumb like a war wound.

While Max retrieved the small first-aid kit Marvin kept in his bathroom, she heard her son and Dusty murmuring to each other.

In the living room, she found Josh leaning against Dusty and staring up at him with adoring eyes.

Don't, she thought. *Don't become attached, son. He's only here for a short while, then he'll be off to chase women and rodeo buckles.*

Squatting in front of Josh, she cleaned the tiny cut with an alcoholic swab. He flinched, glanced up at Dusty and straightened his little shoulders.

While a young man's influence on her son might be good, Josh's hero worship of Dusty worried her.

Josh needed a steady influence.

After applying ointment and a bandage, Max returned the kit to the bathroom and stopped back in the front room.

"You coming, Josh?"

"I'll stay here with Dusty."

With a look, she asked a question of Dusty.

"He's good here," he responded to her nonverbal concern. "He can stay until I get tired."

"I'll let Marvin know where you are," Max told Josh and left the house unsettled and wary.

Chapter 8

Dusty watched her go, his emotions an odd jumble of compassion and irritation, but not with the boy.

He liked Josh.

Max's obvious reluctance to leave Josh here alone with Dusty bothered him.

Did she think he would hurt the kid?

Shame on her.

Anyone who knew Dusty for more than a few seconds knew he could no more hurt a child than cut off his own arm.

Not intentionally, at any rate.

How about unintentionally, Dusty?

He didn't know what he meant by that. How would he hurt the boy without meaning to?

He looked down at Josh, who watched him almost adoringly.

The answer came quickly. He could hurt Josh by getting to know him and then by disappearing at the end of August, once the fair and rodeo were over.

Nothing would stop Dusty. Not a stubborn ranch owner, or her endearing son, who even at this moment wiggled his way under Dusty's defenses with his lively, innocent chatter.

Dusty *would* head out to the next job and the next rodeo.

For how long, Dusty?

For as long as I want.

When his psyche pointed to his knee and laughed at his hubris, Dusty chose to ignore it.

"You want to help me make phone calls?" He explained to Josh the importance of the calls. Getting people to participate in the Western events wasn't hard—they were more than happy to do bronc busting and barrel racing. Getting them to enter the polo match while they were here proved more difficult.

He phoned more rodeo riders. Josh listened and occasionally piped in with a great comment or two.

His little voice, audible despite not actually speaking into the phone, softened the hard line of the listeners.

A couple of times, Dusty said, "You're listening to the voice of the future."

And lo and behold, some of the people were swayed and agreed to come.

Max went about her business until late afternoon, when she remembered she should be taking care of her injured employee.

She'd told Charlie she would, and she respected the other woman enough to keep her word.

Damn and blast. She didn't have time for this.

Max headed toward Marvin's house and entered quietly. If Dusty napped she didn't want to awaken him.

In the doorway of the living room, she halted, both pleased and chagrined by the sight in front of her.

Dusty lay on the sofa in his T-shirt and a pair of underwear, his long muscular legs bare. His sweatpants lay on the floor beside the sofa.

Eyes closed and unaware that she watched, he massaged his thigh, long fingers trying to reach around the back to his hamstring. Pain etched commas at the sides of his mouth. His teeth bit into his bottom lips.

A wave of sympathy burst through her. She blurted, "I can do that for you."

His eyes snapped open, pinning her with a pain-hazed glare.

She frowned. "Haven't you been taking your pain medication?"

"Don't like to take it. Fogs my mind."

"You mean Marvin went to the trouble of getting the doctor out here and picking up your prescription and you won't take it?"

"I take it at night. During the day, I need a clear head for work."

Oh. He had a point. Working was good.

The organization of the rodeo hung over Max's head like a burden she really didn't need. It mattered to her. It had to be done.

As a child the annual fair had been her home away from home every summer for the two weeks it stayed open.

Her motivation for getting out of the house had been huge. Mighty. She shivered to think about it now.

Thank God she'd been a kid with backbone and ingenuity.

"How are the phone calls going?" she asked.

"I've got another of my buddies coming out." He told her how Josh's innocent comments really helped.

"Are these guys giving a firm commitment?"

"Yeah. I also got three maybes."

"Those don't do us a bit of good."

"I know. I told them so, but they weren't willing to commit."

She bit her thumbnail. "Are we going to have enough cowboys come out to participate?"

Dusty attempted a reassuring glance, but his face registered too much pain to make it believable.

"Know what, Max?"

"No. What?"

"We have enough for one team. No extras, but we just might be okay."

Max's hopes scooted up out of the bottom of her nervous stomach. "Really?"

"Yep. Steadily, each day, I get at least another guy willing to commit."

She smiled. A laugh burst out of her. "Thank you."

Dusty stared for a moment before looking away. "Did you mean it?"

He looked so hopeful she faltered. Just when she had a firm grip on her hardheadedness toward him, he said things that made her soften. The earnestness in his blue eyes eased her resentment.

She'd lost track of the conversation. "Mean what?"

"Did you mean that you would massage my leg? It hurts like hell."

"Doesn't it hurt when you touch it?"

"Yeah, but massage will stretch out the hamstring and help it to heal faster."

She swallowed. Touching his thigh? Oh, so tempting and so hard, her offer impetuous and the thought of touching him too real.

She had offered. She had no choice but to follow through. She pretended a nonchalance she didn't feel.

"Sure. I can do that."

Her voice might sound confident, but her slow steps betrayed her fear. Only to herself, she hoped.

He lay back with his eyes closed and an arm across his forehead, his features distorted by discomfort.

Funnily enough, she wanted to ease his suffering.

She touched his leg, the hair-dusted skin warm.

Bending forward and curling her fingers around to the back of his thigh, she rubbed.

"This isn't going to work," she said.

He opened his eyes, slow to comprehend. "What?"

"A ten- or fifteen-minute massage like this will kill my

back. There's no room for me to sit beside you. I need you lying down on your stomach."

"Okay." With an effort, he sat up. "Let's go to the bedroom."

The phrase jarred. She'd heard it only once before in her life and it had gotten her into a whole lot of trouble.

This was different. There was nothing even remotely sexual about this. It was purely about helping Dusty to heal.

A funny, pathetic little part of her grieved that it was not sexual, that she was not a woman who knew her way around men and relationships and could just take a man to bed purely for finding him attractive.

Forcing herself to be objective and professional, just an employer helping out an injured employee, she hardened her defenses. She gave her traitorous libido, normally so full of common sense, a good talking-to.

Max knew how disappointing sex was.

Somehow, she knew that wouldn't be the case with Dusty. So what?

He needed a therapeutic massage. Nothing else.

Pull yourself together, Max, she scolded for the entire length of the hallway, with Dusty halting and slow behind her on his crutches.

Longest walk of her life.

She had to get this done quickly, finish all of this tempting touching, and get out of here.

In the bedroom, Max smoothed out the covers. The bed had been made, but clumsily, Dusty doubtless hampered by his injury.

She reached for his crutches, trying hard not to devour his legs with avid hunger. Beautiful like the rest of him, long and proportioned perfectly, they made a visual feast.

Of course they were perfect.

This was Dustin Lincoln, after all. God of male perfection.

He was beautiful. In his pain, he was also oblivious to anything she might be thinking, thank goodness.

He lay face down on the bed. A sigh gusted out of him.

She put her fingers to his skin and another, longer sigh whispered onto his pillow.

At first, she kept her touch soft, but Dusty said, "Use more pressure. Stretch that hamstring. Please." His voice came out thin.

Her compassion kicked in.

She pressed harder and he moaned. She backed off.

"It's okay," he said. "It hurts, but you aren't doing damage. It's exactly what that hamstring needs."

She dug in, not too hard and not too soft, the experience of her hands on a man's skin strange and unfamiliar.

Her knowledge of men limited, she felt her lack of worldliness while touching a man easy with the opposite sex.

Never had she had a chance to explore a man's body.

Her time spent with men had given her a disgust of many of them and of their bodily demands.

Her stepfather had been—

She shuddered away from those thoughts.

Nope, nope, nope, don't go there. It doesn't belong here in this room.

Then there'd been Josh's father.

Joel had been selfishness personified. He'd wanted to sleep with her. He'd waged a campaign. She'd given in to the temptation to know, just to *know*, a man.

Curious about what all the fuss had been about, she'd wanted to experiment with the physical, to hold a man's body and to have him inside of her.

Her disappointment after a wet, sweaty, noisy, awkward and uncomfortable encounter had been profound.

Maybe she should have chosen a man instead of a boy for her one and only night with a male. At twenty-one, Joel had been only two years older than her.

The second he'd found out about the pregnancy, he'd offered to do the right thing, but had been killed by a bull soon afterward.

Pregnant and rattled by morning sickness that lasted all day every day, Max watched when the bull stomped on Joel, ending her hope for a normal family.

He'd never even met his son.

Thank goodness his father had been a good man.

Max's stepfather sure hadn't been good.

How many other men have you been giving it away to?

The ugliness of his reaction and his accusation had never left her.

She rubbed Dusty's hamstring, his muscled leg real and solid. The hair on his legs abraded her fingers. It felt good. He felt good.

Despite how much she complained about him, and how much she needed to believe him a feckless guy, she knew she fooled herself.

He had a reputation on the rodeo circuit as a hard worker. She wouldn't have hired him otherwise. She'd done her research.

Despite what she thought of as his arrogance with women, his sweetness appealed to her.

Deep inside of her where her woman's intuition resided, she knew he would never leave a woman dissatisfied.

He would be generous in his attentions.

How on earth would that feel, to have all of his famed charm turned to her and her body?

Sweat dribbled between her breasts.

An image flashed through her of his strong hands, their

backs dusted with soft blond hair, covering her breasts. Of his fingers caressing her nipples.

At the thought, they went hard.

Stop!

What's gotten into you, Max?

Quit thinking inappropriate thoughts.

She fought her burgeoning attraction, those uncomfortable feelings that would only get her into trouble.

He made no bones about the rodeo circuit being his life.

He would never settle down here on her ranch.

She had to resist. Damned hard to do when she touched him so intimately, running her hands all the way up to, but just shy of, a solid buttock.

She'd been too long without a man. Dusty's body was a revelation.

Joel had been a rangy, randy boy.

Dusty was a man.

As skittish as an unbroken horse when she had to deal with men outside of business, Max had never learned the art of flirtation or carefree dalliance.

She didn't know what to *do* with men.

Her life was perfect without them.

But sometimes, late at night, she wanted to hold someone. She wanted to be held. Holding led to all of the other unpleasant stuff, though.

No, thanks.

She rubbed the back of Dusty's leg, applying pressure with her thumbs to stretch his injured hamstring.

It did butterfly-type things to her insides.

Her tummy felt like it rumbled from hunger, but made no sound.

Flustered, she shifted away from Dusty so her hip wasn't touching the side of this leg.

Max sweated with exertion, but mainly with desire for Dusty, a man she didn't really like.

How strange was that?

She had to stop touching him.

Opening her mouth to tell him she'd bring him dinner later, she realized he was asleep.

Tenderness usually reserved for her son washed through her. Dusty trusted her enough, and felt so comfortable with her, that he would actually fall asleep. So sweet.

Without thinking, she did what she would have done with Josh. She brushed a lock of hair away from his forehead.

She placed his crutches close if he needed them.

Smoothing her fingers along his thigh, she stepped away from the temptation of the prettiest male body she'd ever seen.

Leaving the room, she grinned.

Dusty would probably croak if he heard himself described as pretty.

Dusty didn't dare move or breathe too deeply.

He pretended to sleep.

He had sensed Max's unease. Given that she didn't want to take care of him, and that she wasn't comfortable touching him, but did it anyway, his respect for her grew.

He'd known her only briefly, but had learned that she did what had to be done no matter the cost to her personally.

When he'd told his mother that he thought Max was damaged, he'd told her the truth.

He'd lied, though, about wanting to have nothing to do with Max and her vulnerabilities.

To himself, he had to admit that Max intrigued him. What would cause a woman to deny happiness to herself?

She had little experience touching a man. That was painfully obvious. Her touch had been tentative at the start. She'd gotten better.

She massaged him with serious intent.

He didn't want to delve deeper into her psyche. At the same time, he wanted to know what had happened to her and cursed himself for his curiosity.

He lived a normal life, happy in his straightforward, simple pleasures. He neither needed nor wanted to get entangled with a troublesome, troubled woman.

No way no how did he want complications.

Complicated was Maxine Porter's middle name.

Another problem presented itself in the erection pressing into the mattress.

How could this woman tempt him and tease him when they barely got along? When she touched him awkwardly, without the least bit of finesse, whether sexual or not?

He didn't find her attractive. He didn't like her. He didn't want to have anything to do with her. He didn't want a relationship. He didn't want a ready-made family.

He didn't make overtures to women who were not available by his definition.

Max had a lot of responsibilities here on her ranch, saddled with worries and too many concerns, and she had a son.

None of those things fit into Dusty's lifestyle.

But his body desired her. Or at least, it desired that those sharp, fine fingers find their way from his injured hamstring to other parts of his body.

Tender, sensitive, longing parts.

Utter foolishness.

He may not know Max well but he trusted his instincts. Max would fall hard once she let herself go.

She didn't dally. She didn't take anything lightly.

Once the woman tore aside all of her restraints, she'd be a passionate lover. Dusty had no doubt about that.

Loyal to a fault, she loved her son, her ranch, Marvin, her friends and her commitment to this damned rodeo and the people of the town of Rodeo, with an intensity Dusty had never tried.

Dusty didn't have it in him to deal with a love of that force.

Who was he kidding?

Why worry?

She didn't think much of him or his lifestyle, so nothing would happen between them.

Dusty would deal with his desire by hiding it from her and keeping his distance in the future.

No more massages.

He pretended to snore, because as much as he loved her touch, he needed her to stop.

She touched his forehead sweetly, brushing hair away from his face.

She gave the back of his thigh one last caress. Yes, unless he missed his guess that was a caress, not the end of a massage.

God. He had to be careful with quirky, passionate Max.

Two days later, Dusty and Max sat in the diner waiting for Sam Carmichael to show up so they could discuss the polo match further.

Dusty had been studying the videos of matches that Marvin had brought back from Sam late in the afternoon of Max's massage.

Damned if Dusty didn't get excited watching them, polo every bit as tough and exciting as rodeo.

Marvin had sat with him after Josh went to bed, and even his resistance had softened.

After one match, they'd stared at each other and Dusty had admitted, "Max might be onto something."

Marvin had nodded.

Now Dusty sat with Max in the diner ready to move ahead with planning the thing.

He shifted on the bench. His hamstring might be better today, but his knee still ached.

After watching the videos, Dusty hoped like hell it would be healed in time to play polo and ride a bull. If it had to happen, he had to be part of it.

Remembering Max massaging his thigh, he stared at her while she ate and wondered about her relationship with Joel.

"What happened with Josh's father?"

Max stared at him, the burger in her hand forgotten. "What do you mean?"

"I mean, was he your one true love? How soon after Josh was born did he die?"

She put her burger down onto her plate carefully and said, "He never met Josh."

"Man, that's tough."

Max chewed on a french fry before agreeing.

"Tell me what happened."

Max wiped her fingers on her serviette. "Joel and I spent only one night together. Josh happened."

"Surprise, surprise," Dusty said.

"Yes. A shock. Joel agreed to do what he considered the right thing."

She stared out the window and her eyes widened. "My stepfather—"

"Your stepfather?" Dusty asked.

"The man kicked me out." She pointed through the window onto Main Street. "Speak of the devil."

Dusty glanced outside. "The guy in the green shirt? He's your stepfather?"

Max nodded.

Whipcord thin, with a bulbous forehead and nose, he

might be the oddest man Dusty had ever come across. Tufts of hair stuck out in an unruly, uneven halo around a receding hairline.

What had Max's mother seen in the man? Gold glinted from his baby finger and from a chain around his neck.

He wore a well-tailored, expensive sport jacket and shirt.

Maybe his allure had been money.

Maybe Max's mother had been looking for security.

The man spotted Max in the window and entered the diner.

Max stiffened.

Dusty went on high alert, strangely protective all of a sudden.

"When can I see my grandson?" the guy asked without preamble. "It's been too long."

"He isn't your grandson."

The man's lips thinned. "He's the closest thing to one I'll ever have."

"Boohoo for you." Max ignored the man and continued to eat.

Dusty sat back, shocked that she would deal with the guy so poorly. In Dusty's world, family loved family. They treated each other with respect.

Her business didn't matter to him, but his curiosity spiked at the hostility invading their table. He'd gathered from Marvin that her stepdad wasn't a stand-up guy.

"I want to see him," the man said. She hadn't introduced the man to Dusty, another indication of Max's displeasure.

Despite being gruff and rough around the edges, Max had good manners. She knew the basics and taught her son accordingly.

The overwhelming animosity coming off her in heated waves spoke volumes about her hatred of her stepfather.

"I demand to see Josh," the guy insisted. Big mistake

to demand anything of Max Porter. "Send him over this weekend."

"No," Max said. "You kicked me out when I was pregnant, remember? You have no rights where Josh is concerned. Stop pestering me, Graham. It isn't going to happen."

Graham stormed out of the diner.

In the quiet vacuum left by the overdose of emotion, Max slowed down on eating her meal.

"Keep eating," Dusty said, knowing that outings were rare for Max and this was his treat. "You need to keep up your strength when dealing with scum."

Her hazel eyes shot to meet his placid gaze.

"How do you know he's scum?"

"By the way you treat him. If you liked the man, or even if you disliked him and yet respected him, you would treat him accordingly."

She huffed out a breath that sounded to Dusty like a sigh of relief.

"Tell me about him," he said.

"Not here. Please."

"Okay. On the drive home."

She nodded.

"So Marvin stepped up to the plate when *he* wouldn't?" Dusty gestured with his head out to Main Street.

"Marvin is a better man than Graham will ever be and more of a father to me than him. When Marvin found out I was pregnant, he was delighted. Then Graham kicked me out of the house and—"

"Your mother *let* him?"

Stillness settled over Max. Her shoulders bowed as though someone had just tossed a heavy cloak over her. "My mom was already dead by then."

Dusty reached across the table and took her hand.

She didn't pull away, and that said a lot about how upset she was.

"So Graham kicked you out and…?"

"And Marvin took me in." Max swallowed hard. "I will never have the words or the means to thank him enough. If he ever gets sick I will nurse him to health. He will have a home with me forever. I will never put him into a nursing home."

Her passion astounded Dusty. He'd suspected that she would be loyal to friends, but the ferocity of her whispered confession stunned him. He didn't doubt for a moment she meant every word.

Marvin would always have a champion named Max in his corner.

"I'm not a big spender," Max said, "and I've worked since I was old enough to do so. I wanted to get out away from…the house."

The house? Or Graham? Suspicions pecked away at him. He didn't like the direction of his thoughts.

"I don't buy much," she continued. "Not clothes or makeup or whatever people spend money on. I like dealing with animals. As a teenager I liked to ride and to ranch and to care for cattle. So I never spent money."

"You saved it up."

"Yes. Then I bought Marvin's ranch. I just barely had enough for a tiny down payment—it's a fair-sized ranch—but the bank allowed what I had. Marvin has a place to live free of charge for his later years."

"And someone who loves him to take care of him."

"Yes. Very much so."

This different side of Max, a quiet one without attitude and animosity, appealed to Dusty. He suspected her hostility sprang out of feeling constantly overwhelmed by short finances and too much duty resting on her shoulders.

Here in the diner for these few minutes away from all of that, she seemed inclined to treat Dusty as a friend and let her guard down.

He liked her without her guard, with a relaxed softness that made him want to wrap his arms around her while they discussed painful topics, to rub her back and tell her it would all work out. He wanted to offer comfort, not in his usual offhand "hey, I can make you feel better, babe" way, but with more compassion.

He'd like to lift her burdens and give her enjoyment. A fun day or weekend or holiday. Or night.

Max's problems were ongoing and chronic. They weren't fleeting and couldn't be solved with a hug.

Sam showed up at that moment.

Dusty swung around to sit beside Max so they could both face Sam. She scooted closer to the window to make room for him.

"Hey, what's up?" Sam signaled to Vy, pantomiming that he wanted a coffee.

She brought it over herself, kissed her new husband and sashayed away with an exaggerated sway of her hips that Sam couldn't tear his eyes away from.

Max cleared her throat and two pairs of male eyes swung their attention to her.

"We need to nail down details about the polo match," she said.

"This is what we have so far." Sam outlined how the ponies were being shipped out and when they would arrive, any day now, how many there would be and who their riders would be.

"These are all your friends?" Dusty asked.

"Friends and acquaintances. One former business colleague." Sam sipped his coffee. "They all have money and they are all willing to spend it here in small-town Montana."

"Will they lord it over the townspeople?" Max asked. "That they're rich and we aren't?"

"One guy, Emory, will. He's a stiff-rumped descendant of ancestors who came over on the Mayflower. Thinks he's better than everyone around him." Sam caught Vy's eye and smiled. "His snobbery is probably why he's currently on his fourth wife."

"Fourth," Max breathed. "What are the other men like?"

"Decent. Hardworking. Some of them have old money and some is newly earned. Either way, what they all have in common is their love of polo and their fierce need to win."

Dusty smiled. He couldn't relate to wealth on that level, but he understood competition like it was imprinted in his DNA.

Sam had carried a book in with him. He plopped it onto the table.

"What's that?" Dusty thumbed through it.

"Everything you ever wanted to know about polo. It covers all of the rules, the objectives, the care of the animals."

Dusty tucked it onto the seat beside him. Bedtime reading.

Sam turned his attention to Max. "How are you doing finding homes for all of our precious ponies?"

"Really well," Max responded. "Ranchers lined up to help out. They're generous people. They are also incredibly interested in the entire business of bringing in the ponies."

"It'll be good for our guys to get a look at the horses they'll be riding." Dusty sipped his coffee.

"They're spectacular," Sam said. "*And* they are the reason you'll be able to pick up the game so quickly."

"What do you mean?"

"Our horses are trained for the job. A really good polo horse can almost do the job alone. Your horses are trained for rodeo events, which is how my guys will have a fair shot competing against you all. They know what needs to be done. Simplistic, maybe, but a bit valid, too."

He glanced at Dusty's crutches. "We might not be able to win each other's events, but maybe we can make a good accounting of ourselves anyway. Even you with your injury."

Dusty nodded. He'd continued to worry about how his cowboys would compete with the city folks. So now he had one more piece of information to share with the rodeo people committed to the polo match.

"Did Sam tell you his ponies are already here?" Vy leaned one hip against their table and rested her free hand on her round belly.

"Already? When can we meet them?" Max sounded like her little son, Josh, all excitement and unbridled curiosity.

"As soon as we finish up here, you can drive out. I have errands to run, but you can head out on your own."

"I'll stop in and say hi to Carson while I'm there."

"Not today, Max. Sorry. He's having one of his bad days. He didn't recognize me this morning."

Max frowned with gentle concern. "Who's with him now?"

"Chelsea."

To Dusty, Sam said, "She's my teenage daughter. She and my granddad have a special bond. He never forgets her name and always knows who she is."

"Dementia?" Dusty asked.

"Alzheimer's." The sadness on Sam's face tore at Dusty.

Sam asked Max questions about the feed that would be provided for the ponies, edging the conversation away from a subject that obviously pained him.

"Samantha Read has given us a budget for their feed."

Sam shook his head. "No. The committee is not paying for this. The owners will pay their own expenses for their own ponies. They all agreed to that."

Max's expression eased. Obviously, any and all financial items for the fair and rodeo concerned her.

Sam's elegant features erupted with a feral grin. "I made sure they agreed to those terms before I let them come here."

"Let them?" Dusty asked. "What do you mean?"

"Because these guys were reluctant and I wasn't sure how many I could convince to come all the way out here, I contacted more players than we had room for."

"You didn't ask them to come out here," Dusty said, wonder in his voice. "You got them competing for the *privilege*."

Sam grinned. Dusty laughed. He had to admire a man who could pull that off.

"It worked," Sam said. "They're covering all of their costs."

To Max, he gave voice to a concern. "I need to know there are enough supplies."

"Plenty," she said. "No worries. We're all good to go as soon as the other ponies start to arrive."

"We?" Dusty asked. "You'll be housing ponies, too?"

She nodded, still looking as excited as her son with the prospect of a late night and popcorn.

"Let's go look at Sam's ponies." She nudged Dusty to get him moving out of the booth and onto his crutches.

Yep, as excited as a little kid.

This relaxed, animated Max charmed Dusty.

He caught a glimpse into her soul, into a part of her that had probably been left behind when Josh came along and she'd been thrown into too much responsibility at too young an age.

He glimpsed a flame that hadn't been completely extinguished.

Chapter 9

Dusty hauled himself into the passenger seat of Max's truck.

Max tossed the crutches into the bed and climbed into the driver's seat.

She pulled out of Rodeo onto the small highway leading to the fairgrounds, a satisfied smile on her face. "Were you happy with today's meeting?" he asked.

She grinned. "I am. I'm glad things are coming together smoothly with the polo match, now that we've got enough players on board." She stared out the windshield. "I know a lot of people doubted it, but I think it's going to work out."

Dusty inclined his head.

Many people were in the habit of underestimating Max—himself included. Still unsure about the outcome of the polo match, he kept his doubts to himself. He wouldn't dampen her spirits.

She leaned one elbow on the open window well and let the warm breeze rush over her. "Nadine's going to write up a series of articles to push the novelty of the whole idea. First one comes out tomorrow."

Silent for a long time, Dusty pounded his fist onto one thigh. "You know," he said, nodding slowly, "I'll admit that despite having concerns, I'm really coming around to the idea."

Max smiled at him, as if to say, *I told you so.*

Dusty ignored her triumphant expression. "Coming around to the idea" didn't mean that he was foolish enough to think it was going to be a blazing success.

"How bad is the hamstring today?" Max asked and Dusty

didn't like the change of subject. He didn't want to be reminded of the injury.

"Not too bad. Painful, but better than the knee." Reluctant to share how much it still hurt, he didn't think he could survive another massage.

"Is it going to affect whether you can participate in the polo match and the rodeo events?"

"Nope." Nothing in Dusty's tone intimated that he wanted to say more.

Max slowed the truck and stared at him.

"Eyes on the road," he said.

"But—"

"The discussion's closed, Max. Move on."

"Fine." She pressed her foot to the gas and they shot forward.

"We're private here," Dusty said. "It's you we should talk about. Spill about Graham. Is it what I think?"

Max's foot hesitated on the gas, but a second later their speed evened out. "Probably, if what you think involves a grown man trying to get into a young teenager's bedroom at night."

Dusty groaned, because that's what he had suspected.

"Do you want to talk about it?" he asked.

"Yes and no. I never have before, but I think Marvin's probably guessed. My friends, too."

She chewed on her bottom lip. "Maybe it's time to talk about it. It's not good to keep things bottled up inside. Maybe it would be therapeutic to get it off my chest."

That word *chest* had him thinking about how she had felt when he'd lain on top of her in the mud. The urge to ask her about it filled him. He tamped down on it.

"You haven't talked to your friends about your stepfather trying to get into your bedroom?"

"No, but they're smart women. I'm sure they've guessed."

"Why me?"

"What?"

"If you haven't talked to them about it, why tell me when you don't even like me?"

She stared at the road ahead for a while before breaking the silence.

"They've had experiences of their own, so I don't like to burden them or risk having their own issues come up to haunt them." Expression thoughtful, she went on, "Even though we're so different, we were drawn together as friends because of shared backgrounds or past experiences, things that happened to us that were the same or similar. So we understand each other."

"Meaning that you've all been abused?"

"In one way or another. Some of us have shared stories more than others."

She tapped her fingers on the steering wheel. "Maybe it's like when soldiers come home from war. They come from different places, but then they're thrown together in a horrendous situation. That experience of war is so profound they never forget it or their link to each other. Maybe in a way it defines them for the rest of their lives."

Not for the first time, Dusty thanked his lucky stars for his normal, uneventful upbringing and his loving home, the severest violence he'd ever suffered a paddling on his butt once for talking back to his mother. He'd never done it again.

There'd never been dark, looming threats in the night, or even darker realities.

"Did Graham ever…?"

"No."

"He tried," Dusty said, a statement, not a question, his tone flat, but with all kinds of emotion behind it. He had no respect for men who preyed on women.

"Yes, he tried often," Max said. "I made sure he didn't succeed."

"By dressing like a boy," Dusty guessed, "and by binding your breasts."

Her mouth fell open. "How did you know?"

"When we slipped in the mud, I fell on top of you. You felt unusual. You know. There."

He glanced at her chest. She caught the look.

A smile tugged at the corner of her mouth. A sudden urge to lick that spot and to kiss her full lips flooded him, to ease her past burdens, to erase the nasty memories Graham instilled in her and give her the happy adolescence she deserved.

"I guess you've had enough experience to know when a woman feels unusual…there." Her smile broadened. Good God, she was pretty.

Dusty grinned. "Yep. Plenty."

The harmony in the vehicle hummed with sunshine and good humor.

Then a thought occurred. "You haven't lived with Graham for, what? Nine years?"

She nodded.

"So why still do it?"

"I—I don't— I can't honestly say. I first started wearing really tight sports bras when I started developing and I guess it became a habit."

"It can't be good for you. I wish you would just be yourself. Be natural."

"I'm glad you said *I wish*." Her voice might have been a bit huskier than usual. He wondered why. "I'm glad you didn't *tell* me how I should be dressing."

"Hey, lady, your body is yours to do with what you want. I just wonder what it's doing to your breasts to hold them so tightly all the time."

The word *breasts* resonated in the cab, turning a confessional conversation suddenly sexual.

Or at least it turned sexual for Dusty because he wondered what they looked like when they weren't fettered, if that was the proper term.

He'd taken to thinking of Max more and more in that way and he just didn't get why. She did nothing to entice him. She rarely smiled, but when she did...whoa. Like sunshine on a mountain lake.

She didn't share much of herself, but when she did... again, whoa. She shared deep and heavy and passionate stuff.

"So just covering yourself up was enough to make Graham keep his hands off?"

"God, no. I barred my door at night. I went out and bought a lock and key. I told him if he ever came in and hurt me I'd tell the sheriff. He laughed at that because the sheriff at the time was his good buddy."

Even though the summer sun shone hot rays through the windows and the cab was close, a chill ran along Dusty's bones to think of a young girl defending herself against a grown-up who had all the power.

"I stayed out of the house after school as long as I could, and when I got home I'd lock the door and shove my dresser against it every night."

She turned on the heat in the cab. Telling action. The sharing of her story made her as cold as he felt hearing it.

"He would unscrew my lock while I was at school, but I had a stash of them that he never found. I would just pull out another one and screw it on."

"He never found your stash? You mean, he looked?"

"Yeah. He was always snooping through my room."

"Where were you hiding them that he couldn't find them?"

"That dresser I moved every night? There was a loose floorboard underneath it. I stored locks in that old cavity."

"Smart."

"I had to be."

His respect for her grew. She was strong, all right. The stubbornness that he found so hard to deal with had gotten her through her adolescence unscathed.

Physically, at any rate.

She'd had to learn early on to be strong-willed.

Thinking of how she frustrated Graham every night, he chuckled.

"Good for you, Max," he said, a world of admiration in his tone. "I'm glad you won against Graham."

She startled and then smiled.

At the Rodeo fairgrounds, Max turned in under the wrought iron arch and drove the length of the grounds to a stable out behind the Carmichael house.

Max threw the truck into Park and bounded out and into the stable, forgetting that Dusty needed his crutches.

"Hey!" he called as he struggled out of the cab.

She returned a second later. "Sorry. I forgot. Oh, my God, you should see the ponies. They're gorgeous."

"I wouldn't mind seeing them if I could have my crutches." Dusty softened that with a wink.

He doubted Max got this exhilarated often.

He followed her into the stable and saw what she meant about the ponies.

There were four of them.

Dusty had already learned that one pony did not play an entire game, so the owners would be bringing in multiples. Hence the need for Max to arrange quarters for them from a number of local ranchers.

"These are expensive horses," Max said, awe in her

voice. "They've got to have Thoroughbred breeding. I'm sure of it. Look at this one."

Dusty look his fill at the most pampered, expensive horses he'd ever seen.

Glancing around, the state of the stable declared that polo was a rich man's sport.

Dusty loved his horse and kept him to the highest standards he could afford, but nothing he could do compared to the renovations Sam had made in this building over the summer.

Air-conditioned and climate controlled for all seasons, as far as Dusty could tell, gave the ponies pampered surroudings.

A small older man sauntered out of a back room. A groom.

Max greeted him. "Hi. I'm Max Porter. This is Dusty Lincoln. Sam said we could come out and meet the ponies."

"I'm Gordie Hugh." He laid a proprietary hand on the door of one of the stalls. "I came out from New York State with the ponies."

"Tell me their names, please. Who is who?" Max bubbled over with goodwill. Gordie reacted to Max's smile with one of his own. He told them about each horse, including names and histories and every idiosyncrasy.

Dusty smiled benignly at the groom, all the while thinking how the man was giving him ammunition to share with his buddies.

Max seemed to have the same idea, as she continued to pepper the groom with questions that he answered readily. He pointed to the pony in the nearest stall. "This is a Thoroughbred quarter horse mix."

Next, he pointed to another. "Thoroughbred and Criollo from Argentina, one of the quickest, most maneuverable horses you'll ever meet."

Dusty checked him over with a knowledgeable and practiced eye. He knew horses well. These were beautiful.

He thought of the horses on the rodeo circuit, including his own, and the ones he'd seen compete this summer.

All fine horses, any one of them could compete against these rarefied creatures.

Dusty would bet on it.

More optimistic than he had been since he'd first arrived in Rodeo and found out about the polo match, Dusty thanked Gordie. He and Max left, with Dusty musing that the groom had underestimated Max in her dull clothes and childlike enthusiasm.

"Think you could take him in a race?" he murmured as they walked to the truck.

"In a heartbeat," she said and her smile had him wanting to weep buckets of happy tears.

They drove home with Max chattering on about the horses, a different person, happy and carefree for these few moments.

He knew some of her truths and her vulnerabilities.

That word—*vulnerabilities*—the same one his mother had used. She'd urged him to dig deeper and he had. Damned if he knew what to do with the information, though.

He didn't plan to fall in love with the woman just because she'd had a hard life and she'd shared her secrets with him.

Why with him?

Okay, he understood Max's thinking about not wanting to bring up old negative feelings in her friends, but he was a stranger.

Maybe that was the reason, though. He wouldn't be hanging around. He had no future here in Rodeo. He wouldn't be here for her to bump into on the street and remember everything she'd told him.

In less than a month he'd be gone.

Back on Max's ranch, he walked to Marvin's house, seriously considering paying Graham a visit and setting ground rules for the future, but that would be paternalistic.

His mom laid that word on his dad one night when they were fighting. Dusty had laughed at his dad's expense until his mom had used it on him a few days later.

His mom educated him, that was for sure.

Max didn't need him to fight her battles for her.

She did need support and help with the rodeo. He could do that for her.

Funny that he didn't resent her as much as when he'd first arrived. Funny how a little confessional conversation turned all parties into goodwill ambassadors.

He walked to the office with a friendly wave toward Max as she headed to the stables.

Dusty was going to wring Max's neck.

If she didn't stop changing the rodeo on him, he would flat-out quit the job, leave and not look back.

It would serve her right if he did just that. Without warning. Without a backward glance.

He'd been pacing in the aisle of the stable, but pulled up short. His agitation riled up the horses.

Now she wanted to have camel racing.

True, just for the children, but come on. Where were they supposed to get camels on short notice?

The object of his anger stomped into the stable.

"What's wrong with you?" she asked, on the offensive. "You walked away from me so rudely."

He'd had to or he really would wring her neck.

"What's wrong with *me*?" One of the horses whinnied. Dusty took Max's arm and steered her outside. "You're the one who keeps changing the itinerary."

"It's not that big a change. We need something for the children."

"Camel racing?"

"It could be fun."

"It could be dangerous. Camels have long legs and they're too high off the ground. Plus, they're fast. If a kid went tumbling off a camel's back he or she could be seriously hurt."

Max chewed on another poor fingernail. She deflated and backed down. "You're right. It is too dangerous. I'm sorry. Dusty, I'm worried."

Mollified, Dusty's anger eased. "I'm surprised you even considered it."

Max wrung her hands. "I'm scared. What if the rodeo is a flop? There's a lot riding on this. The future of the town is at stake."

"You can't think like that. Stop it now."

She stared at him. "Okay. No worrying. The rodeo is going to be a raging success."

Dusty laughed out loud. When Max reverted to sarcasm, he actually liked her.

"I've come around to liking your polo match idea," he said. "I have no reservations left."

Max's eyebrows shot up. "Really?"

"Yeah, really. Selling this as a battle between cowboys and city dwellers should make for a lot of fun. It gives this rodeo a unique aspect. People will be curious. They'll come with a super derisive bias, and a lot of tickets will be sold because of that, but they'll end up having a good time. I think— You know, I really think it was a brilliant idea."

A smile that started as a slow-moving dawn spread to the heat of high noon across her lips. God, she had a pretty smile.

He liked that he'd put it there on her face at this moment.

"Okay, the polo match is good."

He nodded.

"The camel racing isn't."

He shook his head.

"How about if it's adult camel racing?"

He'd ride a camel in a heartbeat. It would be fun, but he didn't know how safe they were, or how manageable, or how easy to corral.

What if one of them got loose on the fairgrounds and hurt someone? He'd heard they like to spit.

Maybe all those concerns could be addressed if the camels came with the right handlers.

"It could work," Dusty said. "Here's the thing, though. You were right that we need to engage the children."

Max chewed on another nail but stopped long enough to say, "It's a family-oriented fair."

"How about a really unique petting zoo? Let me ask around to see if anyone I know owns exotic animals."

When Max would have objected, he raised a hand. "*Safe* animals. No wild cats. I'm talking baby llamas. Baby alpacas. Angora bunnies. That kind of thing."

Max brightened and her finger fell from her mouth. "I know a woman who owns pygmy goats. They're the cutest little things and they love attention. I'll call her."

"We'll make this work," Dusty said. At the thought of the cute animals they could gather for the kids, he got excited. This rodeo could actually succeed! Grabbing Max, he kissed her on the cheek.

Max's eyes got huge.

He felt his own follow suit.

What— He—

Faster than a jackrabbit could skedaddle away from a fox, Dusty scooted to Marvin's house, all consideration for his poor hamstring forgotten in his haste to get away.

His cheeks burned hotter than he could remember in

years. The last time he'd blushed so hard had been in sixth grade when he'd kissed Ashley Baker behind the school and she'd promptly said, "Yuck," smashing his youthful pride.

He'd gained a lot of skill since then, but kissing Max, even just her cheek, had never been his intention.

What the heck had he been thinking?

Max stared at Dusty's retreating back.

She didn't know what to think of what had just happened.

A flirtatious guy, maybe Dusty had just been overcome by the joy of the moment and had acted the way he would with another woman. *Any* other woman. A woman other than Max.

She resisted the urge to touch her cheek.

His lips on her skin had felt…amazing.

Oh, stop it, Max. You have more sense than to be taken in by Dusty Lincoln.

Yes, she did, but she'd also really, really liked the feel of his lips on her cheek.

She imagined his lips elsewhere on her skin and her body heated.

She walked away dazed. Oh, definitely dazed.

The polo ponies arrived.

Dusty limped out to the yard like an animated ten-year-old. The four horses being unloaded from a trailer were to be stabled on Max's ranch.

Sam Carmichael came over with Vy, along with a couple men Dusty didn't recognize but who had the same polished moneyed look that Sam did.

Max scowled at the men.

Had one of the men said something inappropriate?

Had one of them insulted her? Or her ranch?

When Dusty got close enough to hear the conversation, he understood why.

"Seriously, Carmichael?" One of the strangers gestured around the yard. "We bring our ponies all the way from New York and *this* is the best you can do to accommodate them?"

Max opened her mouth, no doubt to deliver a blistering response, but Dusty put his hands on her shoulders and squeezed. He didn't want to pull the macho "I'll take care of this" card, but Max had hired him to organize the rodeo. He was responsible for making it a success.

And she was about to insult the men who were putting up serious money to be here.

Max wanted a polo match, so she would get her polo match, but only if she kept her mouth shut and didn't offend the sponsors.

"Have you looked in the stables?" Dusty directed the question to the guy who'd spoken.

He turned a superior eye on Dusty and tried to look down his nose at him. Too bad Dusty was a good four inches taller than the man.

Dusty stuck out his hand. "Dustin Lincoln."

The guy had no choice but to shake hands or show himself badly to the locals. "Emory Blake."

Ah. The guy Sam had warned them about. The one with the snobbish attitude.

"We had a conference call," Dusty said. "You, Max and me."

"Yes. So we did." He glanced around the yard again. "Tell me why I should look in the stables."

"In Montana, we don't judge a ranch by the outer trappings, but by the state of their cattle. Come look at the Porter horses. Then tell me what you think of the care your ponies will get here."

Sam shot him an approving nod.

Inside, the stable showed well, as impeccably clean as ever.

Curious horses bent their heads over stall doors.

Emory Blake and the other man, who introduced himself as Peter Force with less antagonism than Blake had, walked the aisles checking the horses.

Dusty knew they were well tended. He'd watched Max baby them enough. He understood why, now that he knew her and her situation better. She couldn't afford to replace them.

Peter nodded. "Their care is above reproach."

At that moment, a whack of straw cascaded from the hayloft.

Max, tone low and displeased, called up, "Josh? What are you doing up there?"

Dusty heard the concern in her voice. She needed to make a good impression. Her rodeo had to come off without a hitch. Despite her reaction to these two men, she had to please them.

"I'm looking at the ponies in our yard, Mom. They're pretty! Can I ride one?"

"No. They aren't ours. Come down from there. Now."

"'Kay."

He climbed down, but jumped when still halfway up. Dusty caught him around the waist so the kid wouldn't land and break an ankle. That would be just what Max needed. More stress.

"Come see my pony." Josh grabbed Emory's hand and dragged him to the end of the aisle. The guy looked distinctly uncomfortable and not at all a kid kind of person. Dusty hid a grin.

"Look!" Josh said. "His name's Cookie, 'cause he really likes oatmeal cookies."

In the presence of Josh's cuteness factor, Emory eased up a bit on the poker face.

"He's a fine specimen."

"He's not a spaceman."

Peter Force, at least a decade younger than Emory and patently more comfortable with children, said, "Emory means he's a great pony. You like to ride?"

"I love it. Mom's going to buy me a horse soon. A big one." Josh peered up between Emory and Peter. "Can I ride one of your ponies?"

"No!" Emory's harsh ejaculation had everyone staring. "I mean, they're expensive."

At Josh's stricken expression, Emory waved a hand in Cookie's general direction. "Not…um…as cute as yours, but…pricey."

Peter placed his fingers on Josh's shoulder. "I'll let you up on one of mine in the corral, but only when I'm present. Okay?"

"'Kay. Thanks."

"Let's get the ponies into their temporary homes," Max said.

Peter moved to accommodate her request, but Emory turned to Dusty. "Where do mine go?"

Dusty needed to nip Emory's arrogance in the bud, and set matters straight.

"Max owns the ranch. I'm merely her employee. She'll take care of you and your ponies." To Sam Carmichael he said, "Can I see you outside for a minute?"

Sam followed him out. "What's up?"

Out of earshot of Emory and Peter, Dusty said, "Nothing. I just needed an excuse to remove myself from the situation in there so Emory will be forced to deal with Max."

"Smart."

"What's his problem? That chauvinism might have passed muster four decades ago, but now?"

"Emory has three ex-wives. They've all taken him to

the cleaners. Not that the arrogant SOB didn't deserve it. The bottom line is that he has a real problem with strong, independent women."

They watched handlers walk the horses around the yard. "What do you think of them?" Sam asked.

"They came here in style. They look like pampered babies."

"Pampered, yes, but don't underestimate them. They're spectacular in motion. They can turn on a dime." He pointed to one of them. "Reba there is the fastest pony you'll ever see run."

"How are we going to work out the logistics of our practice sessions? We'll get to know each other's flaws and strengths."

"Good question. You have any ideas?"

"I'm thinking we'll have to use the fairgrounds at different times and be on our Scout's honor to not spy."

"I can totally trust the cowboys to do that."

"But not the city boys?"

"Not a chance." Sam smirked. "I'll see what I can do with them and what kind of promises I can wring out of them."

"Either that or keep them busy."

"That's a possibility."

"They need to practice barrel racing anyway."

Max led the two men and her son out of the stable to begin the process of getting the ponies settled in.

"Who owns Reba?" Dusty asked.

"Emory."

"How is he as a rider?"

"Not as good as he thinks, but a force to be reckoned with nonetheless once he's on her."

"And Peter?"

"Good. Damned good."

Dusty stared at Sam. "And you?"

Sam lowered his lashes and said, with a show of modesty, "Pretty good."

"Meaning damned good, like Peter."

Sam burst out laughing. "I'm better than Peter."

Dusty grinned. "Glad we got that settled."

He checked out his competition, guessing Peter to be in his early thirties and Emory in his midforties.

Peter had a lean, fit physique that looked strong. Emory, on the other hand, had arrogance and force of personality on his side, neither of which Dusty would underestimate, but he looked soft around the middle.

If Emory didn't stand a chance of winning, he wouldn't be here. Dusty didn't know the man, but he sensed that Emory didn't put himself into situations in which he might experience the possibility of failure.

Except marriages, apparently.

It looked like Dusty had his work cut out for him.

Both men had a combative streak that emanated from them in the way they walked and how they handled their ponies.

Sam was right. They liked to win.

"We might be an amateur league," Sam said, "but we mean business."

"Yeah, I'm getting that."

Dusty entered the stable to help Marvin and Max with pony chores.

A welling of ambitious spirit arose in him upon seeing the animals in person.

He wanted to ride one of these ponies, he wanted that match and he wanted to win.

Chapter 10

The following afternoon, Dusty entered the stable to check on the ponies.

All morning, he'd been on the phone to the rodeo riders who'd agreed to try polo riding. He'd been raving about the ponies.

These people knew Dusty wouldn't rave unless he meant it.

Most of them were arriving on the weekend to start practicing polo. That would give them two weeks until the match at the end of the month to whip the rodeo team into shape.

Dusty wanted a closer look at the horses.

He knew the stable was empty. Emory and Peter were at the diner having lunch with Sam.

Max was out somewhere doing chores on the ranch.

Dusty had already plowed through the polo book Sam had given him, and he now knew more about goals and chukkas and mallets and polo ponies and referees than he ever needed to know.

Apparently, the city boys were flying a couple of highly qualified referees out the night before the match.

He felt more confident that he and his buddies stood at least a chance of showing well, if not winning.

Winning might be unrealistic, but entertaining the crowd could be done.

Peter's pony was a fine beauty, if a bit skittish.

He moved to Emory's pony, Reba, and found her every bit as full of herself as her owner.

Dusty heard something, a hint of sound from the loft.

Josh?

He started climbing the ladder. "Hey, buddy, I thought you were out with Marvin. What are you doing up here?"

It wasn't Josh.

Max sat with her back to him, swiping her fingers across her cheeks.

He realized what he'd heard. A sob and sniffling.

He'd invaded her privacy.

Awkward.

He should leave.

He didn't want to.

Rather, he wanted to delve, to dig deeper as his mother had urged. True, she'd meant that he should be looking more deeply into himself and what he wanted in life, but at the moment he would say Max needed a friend.

Scrambling across the straw, he sat down behind her. The loft looked like a young boy's dream. Max kept it clean for him. A big clear plastic bin in the corner held blankets that Josh could use with his sleeping bag when he ran away once a month, along with bags of potato chips and cans of ginger ale.

If ever he'd wanted proof of Max's love and abilities as a mother, it was this safe haven for her son.

But why was Max crying?

It seemed to Dusty that she'd been under tremendous stress since the day he'd arrived on her ranch. What more could have happened that was the straw that broke her back?

He reached out a hand to touch her, but thought better of it.

"Talk to me," he said, as soothingly as he thought Max might talk to Josh if he was upset.

"I ca-a-an't."

"Why not?"

"I'm being silly. I'm being emotiona-a-al. I'm weak."

"And?"

"And I need to be strong."

"Always?"

"Yes. Josh needs me. Marvin needs me. I've taken a huge chance on the polo match." She spun around, sending straw flying, and threw herself into Dusty's arms.

He wasn't expecting it and barely caught her, but once he did, once he had her wrapped in his arms, he liked her there.

He rubbed a hand along her spine.

"Oh, Dusty, I've been arrogant and foolish. That stupid snotty Emory makes me feel so awkward and...and... awkward. We've spent a year and a half pulling this revived fair together and I might ruin the whole thing by deviating from the standard rodeo."

"You might," Dusty said.

"Ohhh. You..." She tried to pull away, but Dusty wouldn't let her. She was strong. He was stronger.

"On the other hand," he said, "you might have a smashing success on your hands. I'm starting to lean toward success."

She pushed away from his chest with closed fists, her nose so bright red, she must have been crying for a while. Poor thing.

Her vulnerability, her softening, made her more attractive, which was nothing he wanted, but Dusty sensed about Max what he should have seen from the start.

Fundamentally, she lived a solitary life, alone and separate. She gave and gave and gave, supported and supported, while she took nothing for herself.

She would hurt herself if she kept on this way and didn't start to take back to refill her well.

Today, she'd hit empty on the gas gauge of her emotions.

She stared at him with wide eyes made luminous by tears. Again, the colors captivated him.

He leaned close, closer, and kissed her, softening his lips

over hers to persuade her to open up to him. He breathed warmth into her, putting as much of his affection and confidence into her as he could.

Her lips relaxed and he deepened the kiss.

When she wasn't scowling or unhappy, she had the prettiest mouth.

She might be unskilled in how she kissed, but her sweet enthusiasm and wonder thrilled him.

He pulled back and ran a finger along her jaw. His hand shook. Max's freshness, that very lack of skill, packed a powerful punch.

Wide-eyed, she stared at him.

"You'll be okay," he said. "I promise."

"Do you really think it can be a success?" she asked, glancing down and ignoring what he'd just done, clearly out of her depth.

Dusty didn't mind. He kinda felt the same way. His hands shook. Him. A guy who felt confident with any woman, but Max Porter... Well, she was unique.

"Yeah, I do." Like her, he stepped away from the impact of that kiss and struggled for an even keel. "The more I look at the ponies, the more I think we can do this. Mainly, though, I want to rub Emory's nose in defeat."

Max emitted a watery laugh, as he'd hoped she might. She curled against him with her head on his shoulder.

Without further sentiments or encouragement, he held her, because it seemed to be all she needed. Just to be held.

He longed to do more to help her, and to make her happy.

He started to form a half-baked, unbelievable idea. A weird idea. She might like it. She might not.

Max had known too little fun in her life. Thanks to her creep of a stepfather, a normal carefree adolescence had been denied her. Then she'd gotten pregnant, at only nineteen if his math was correct.

An uncontrollable urge to help her, to please her and make her happy, filled Dusty. He had to make a fun night happen for her, even if only once.

Even if only to bring her out of this blue funk so she could make it through the rodeo.

He'd like to give her what many teenaged girls experienced as a normal part of growing into womanhood.

It would take planning to set up exactly what he wanted to give her.

"Max?"

"Hmm?" She sounded drowsy. He wondered if she was getting any sleep at all at night or if she tossed and turned with worry.

"Do you want to borrow my mother?" he asked.

"What do you mean?"

"It's possible you need a woman to talk to. The kind who is nurturing and wise. A mother." *And I have to go prepare a surprise.*

"Would she mind talking to me?" Max sounded so sweetly hopeful it melted Dusty's heart.

"She would love it if you would call her. Seriously. Mom loves being needed and I need her so seldom these days. She rues the day I grew up."

Max giggled.

Surprised, Dusty glanced down at her. Tough Max giggling. Strange…and cute.

He held out his hand palm up. "Give me your phone."

She pulled it out of her breast pocket and passed it to him.

He loaded his mom's number in and then called her, handing the phone to Max when it rang.

His mom answered and Max said shyly, "Charlie? Can I talk to you?"

Even without his ear to the phone, he heard his mom's

effervescent response, "Of course, sweetie. What's up?" and Dusty knew Max was in good hands.

He left and limped to his truck for a drive into town to pick up a few supplies.

"Max, wake up. It's me."

Max awoke in the middle of the night slowly to a dark silhouette hovering over her bed who spoke with Dusty's voice.

"Dusty?"

"Yeah, it's me," he whispered. "Are you awake?"

"I am now. What are you doing here?" She rubbed her eyes. "You shouldn't be in my bedroom."

"I know. Sorry about that, but if I'd told you about this ahead of time you wouldn't have agreed to do it."

"Agreed to do *what*?" Her frustration level soared through the roof. She was tired and cranky and afraid that the rodeo would flop, and Dusty had the nerve to sneak into her bedroom and wake her from much-needed sleep.

Plus, she was super embarrassed that he'd caught her crying this afternoon. Crying, for Pete's sake. Oh, the humiliation of him seeing her weakness.

On the other hand, he'd given her a beautiful gift. He'd loaned her his mom. She'd had a wonderful conversation with Charlie and had come away less scared.

She'd been given motherly advice today and it had been the best thing to happen to her in years.

"Dusty, why are you here in my room in the middle of the night?"

Dusty tossed back her covers.

He was lucky she wore pajamas to bed or she would be screaming in earnest.

What was the fool up to?

"Get dressed," he said.

"No way am I going anywhere. I'm tired—"

He pressed one finger against her lips. "I know, but you need to have some fun. Let's go do that."

"I don't need fun. I need sleep."

He wrapped his fingers around the back of her neck, kissed her lips oh-so-lightly and ran his mouth along her jaw to her ear.

Shivery spots of delight followed his lips. What was he doing and why? Oh! He'd nipped her earlobe. It felt good.

What was he—

"Trust me," he whispered.

Goose bumps pebbled her skin where moisture from his mouth lingered, marking her with the softest, gentlest of tattoos. *Whoa.* "Oh…trust you. Okay. I guess. What are we doing?"

He pointed to the star-studded sky outside her window. "Going for an adventure. Are you up for it?"

"What kind of adventure?" she asked, her heart at once both wary and yearning.

"The best," he said and stood with his fingers tucked into his blue jeans' pockets and his cowboy hat tipped back on his head.

A rugged, handsome cowboy stood in her bedroom in the night tempting her with his big body, starlight and the promise of fun.

When had that ever happened to her before? Well…never.

He waited, leaving her to make her decision and come freely.

When had she last had a good adventure, one that didn't involve stress and worry?

What was Dusty up to? What was she agreeing to?

Did it matter?

Her life was all about work and more work.

Why not take a night off?

Moonlight beckoned.

Starlight twinkled.

Dusty tempted.

Fluffy, unfamiliar flutters of the deepest longings welled up in her chest.

She needed...

Dusty must have felt her wavering because he turned his back. "Get dressed. Hurry."

And she did, rushing into her bra and panties. She covered those with her old jeans and a cotton shirt.

When she would have walked to the door, he stopped her and gestured toward the open window, where the top of a ladder rested on the sill.

"We're going out that way," he said.

"Through the window? Why?"

"Because, as I already told you—" he affected a look of exaggerated patience "—you need to have fun."

Sneaking out of the house through the window? Down a ladder?

Yeah, she could do that.

He stepped out and onto the top rung.

"I'll go first in case you fall."

She scooted over to follow. "I won't fall. Anything you can do, I can do better, buddy."

He chuckled. She shushed for him to be quiet. "Are you sure you can do this, with your knee?" she asked, turning serious for a moment.

He smiled at her. "Think I can manage, but I'll go slow and steady, just in case."

"Let's go, then." Her heart set up a happy pounding. This "sneaking out of the house" business was fun.

A couple of rungs from the bottom of the ladder, he stopped her with a hand on the small of her back.

"I won't let you down," he said.

What did he mean? She jumped to the ground.

Stepping onto cool grass, she realized she'd forgotten about socks and shoes.

She hadn't run barefoot through the grass in years. A cliché, yeah, but, dear God, it felt good.

She'd been crammed chock-full to the brim with cares and responsibilities for too many years.

Dusty grabbed her hand and they raced along the yard toward Marvin's house, where Dusty's truck waited.

He shoved her into the passenger seat and pushed the door closed with the barest *click*.

Max had never experienced the carefree delight of sneaking out of the house in bare feet in the dark for an illicit date with a boy.

Dusty started the engine and pulled away from the yard quietly. He drove out across Max's fields.

His hand settled on her thigh, warm and heavy. A man's hand, on her thigh, in the close-quartered cab of a pickup truck, in the darkness.

Heaven.

She waited for his next move. Whatever it might be, somehow she knew she was along for the full ride.

He parked in the middle of a field and put on the hand brake.

"Get out," he ordered.

She did, loving the feeling of discovery, of holding her breath in expectation.

"Come here." He stood at the back of the truck, let down the tailgate and climbed into the bed. "Come on up."

She followed him onto a couple of old handmade quilts softening the hard metal of the bed. He must have raided Marvin's closets.

She sat down, curling her bare feet under her thighs.

He opened a picnic basket. Where on earth had he found it?

A picnic in the bed of a pickup truck, in the middle of a field, in the middle of the night. The surprises kept on coming.

Max smiled.

Oh, Dusty, I am loving this.

If she didn't know better, Max would think Dusty was bent on seduction.

He snapped the top off a lime cooler and handed it to her.

Her eyes widened.

Oh, myyyy. Quilts. Coolers. Was that a container of chocolate-covered strawberries on the blanket? He *did* intend seduction.

Her excitement shot through the stratosphere to play hide-and-seek with the stars.

"Are you okay?" he asked, and she understood what he was really asking.

Did she agree with what he had in mind?

She'd missed all of this in high school, so she didn't know how it worked, but if Dusty *wasn't* intent on seducing her, she would be very, very disappointed.

Her one and only experience of sex had been painful, wet and disappointing.

Surely Dusty would know how to do it better than Joel ever had.

The thrill of anticipation ran along her nerves like water bubbling up from a hot spring.

All of her unrealized yearnings built up over the years, and brought down by disappointment after disappointment, bloomed in her with renewed hope. When would another chance, another opportunity, another Dusty come along? Her younger self, still inside of her after all of these years, yelled, "Go! For! It!"

"Yes," she said, that simply.

In the moonlight, Dusty's smile was neither triumphant

nor smug, but quiet. This wasn't about what he could get *from* her, but what he could give *to* her.

Tonight was all about her.

She couldn't remember the last time that had happened. Her brain, body and heart turned to mush.

Oh, Dusty.

He opened a can of chocolate fondue sauce and set out a container of apple and pear slices. Max suspected that in daylight she would probably see they'd started to brown.

She didn't care.

Everything delighted her, including moonshine alighting on Dusty's thatch of dirty-blond hair.

She would feast on memories of this night for years to come.

He dipped a fruit slice and handed it to her.

She tried to take it from him, but he wouldn't let her.

"Allow me," he said. He held it near her mouth. She opened her lips and tasted chocolate, soft and sweet against tart apple when she bit down.

His finger brushed her bottom lip. She shivered.

He tossed the rest of the slice into his own mouth.

Max stared.

He's sharing my spit, she thought. *He's sharing my germs.*

Her gaze fell to his teeth shining white in the starlight.

Yes! Yes, let's share spit.

She sipped her cooler and shivered again.

"Cold?" he asked. "Come here."

When she didn't move, he grasped her around the waist and lifted her onto his lap, putting her legs on either side of his hips.

He was moving fast.

Too fast?

She thought not.

"What are you doing?" she asked. She didn't understand

the games men and women played. She didn't want to *assume* that Dusty had brought her out here to do…stuff… with her. She didn't think he even liked her, so she needed to know.

But what other purpose would he have? He'd just snuggled her onto his lap, with her private parts nestled firmly against his.

And didn't his private parts feel superb?

He leaned against the side of the truck and took a long, slow pull on his cooler. "Drink up," he said when he swallowed and she watched his throat move. She'd never seen anything more erotic than Dusty swallowing.

She needed to get out more.

She sipped her drink and it chilled her again.

He slipped his hard arm around the back of her waist and pulled her closer.

He dipped a pear slice and held it to her mouth. She bit into it.

Instead of eating the rest, he dipped it again.

Double-dipping. For shame.

He pressed the chocolate-covered fruit to the hollow at the base of her throat.

She gasped. He nudged her chin with his. Her head fell back.

He licked the chocolate from her skin.

"Having fun yet?" he asked, voice husky.

"Yes!" she squeaked.

He raised his lips to hers.

Dusty Lincoln kissed with a slow thoroughness that left her mind hazy and her body limp.

Only his updrawn knees against her back kept her from swooning onto the quilt like a deflating soufflé, in boneless sensual overload.

Oh, sweet heavenly merciful sensual…sex.

And all he had done was kiss her.

Whatever came next just might kill her.

She fell onto him as though he were chocolate cake and potato chips and vanilla sundaes all rolled into one.

His lips persuaded and nibbled and tickled. They ate at her mouth as though she, homely little Maxine Porter, was the most delicious woman on the planet.

His tongue explored, tasting her and taking her mouth as though it belonged to him.

Maybe it did. She no longer knew where she ended and he began.

She'd never French-kissed a man who had so much skill.

She did now, her tongue making enthusiastic forays into his wet, warm mouth. He stilled, giving her access and patience, as though to say, "We have all night."

All night would be good. Awesome. The best.

She licked and withdrew then licked again.

He tasted sweet, like maybe he'd had lemon meringue pie for a bedtime snack.

The man was hopeless. Undiscipli—

His tongue entered her mouth forcefully this time. He'd finished playing games and wanted to get down to business.

But she liked the games. She wanted more of them.

He unbuttoned her blouse.

Oh! Getting down to business was good, too. Fine. Better than fine.

Yes. Let's do it. Let's get down to business.

His fingers full of tender caresses and pressing forays past the pesky restraints of plain cotton slid onto her skin.

Oh, his beautiful, long, *knowing* fingers.

He'd known a lot of women. He'd figured out what they liked.

She reveled in his experience. It taught her the beauty of sensual delights.

"More," she whispered and he laughed.

"I take it that's a yes?"

"That is a definite yes."

He pulled back to meet her eyes. "To everything?"

"I want it all."

A slow grin glimmered in the moonlight.

She should wipe that smugness out of him, his smile full of such pure male confidence, but maybe later. After he touched her some more. After he touched her a *lot*.

"Let's get rid of this," he whispered.

"What?"

"This thing that's restricting you."

Her sports bra.

She wiggled her shirt from her shoulders and arms, and lifted the white restricting bra over her head.

He whistled. "You've been hiding treasures."

Her cheeks warmed. Dusty was only the second man in her lifetime to have seen her breasts. She liked the way he looked at her in the dim moonlight.

Her nipples peaked in the open air.

The master of sensual enchantment whispered his breath over her bare breasts.

He blew on her and she gasped.

"Ohhhhh, yessss."

His lips on her breast curved up and she knew he was smiling.

"I like when you do that," he said.

"Do what?"

"Enjoy."

Oh, it was so much more than mere *enjoying*, but she didn't have the words.

She gave herself over to feeling.

Dusty's callused fingers abraded her soft skin and set up shivery delights all over her breasts.

Goose bumps arose on her arms amid the trembles he started in her when he dipped his forefinger into the chocolate sauce and spread it on her nipple.

When he licked it off her, she just about arched to the stars.

His fingers slipped inside the waistband of her jeans.

When she moved to unzip them he stopped her.

"Not yet."

His fingers delved past the denim and into her panties. The backs of them touched her there, flicking over her hair, the barest whisper of a touch. Back and forth. Back and forth.

She got all hot and achy.

Her eyes flew open and, that moment, she got it.

She understood what Dusty was doing.

He was copping a feel.

He was pretending they were teenagers stealing hot summer delights. He was gifting her with all of the forbidden, stolen secrets she'd been robbed of as a lonely, scared adolescent.

Hence stealing out of the house and the pickup truck, the chocolate he'd dabbed on her nipples, the coolers—coolers! As though Dusty would ever order one in a bar.

When she pushed back on his shoulders so she could see his face, his dimple made an appearance. She imagined him as a teenager, as many young girls would have seen the callow charmer years ago while he learned his art.

In that moment, she fell in love with the man who understood her and with the boy he pretended to be to give her experiences she'd missed.

Tenderness washed through her.

He would never be hers to keep. She understood that, but he was hers for tonight, and it would be enough.

She gave herself over to the adventure.

While he watched her face, he slipped one finger inside of her and she was lost. All she knew was Dusty and the endless firmament of wonder above and around them.

Sex with Dusty Lincoln was spectacular...and it had barely begun.

He cherished her.

She might be the only woman on earth, certainly at this moment the only woman as magnificently and thoroughly loved as a woman could be.

She helped him with the condom and he entered her body, where he felt like the most delicious part of her. Where their bodies bonded as though they belonged together.

They played for a couple of hours.

When she'd reached her third climax, Max *got* it. Finally. She understood what all of her friends had been raving about over the years.

She got the fun. She got the passion. She got the exquisite sensations and the beauty of a man and a woman's body linked together in intimacy.

She got orgasms.

She got sex.

Turning her attention to exploration, because she'd never seen a more beautiful body than his, she wanted to know it all.

She touched, tasted and reveled.

Dawn sent a chill through her.

Pink crested the horizon.

"Thank you," she whispered, her voice echoing the depth of her emotion, trying to convey a gratitude she could never adequately express.

She lay boneless against his chest.

"Was it fun?" he asked, his tone surface light, and she understood. Dusty didn't like to delve. He didn't do heavy or emotional.

After all the gifts he'd given her in the past few hours, she could accept that.

"More fun than I've ever had in my whole life," she said and meant it.

They crept back to the house.

Max didn't want the night to end. She sensed that Dusty didn't want that, either, which was a nice surprise.

"Ladder or front door?" he asked.

"Definitely the ladder." She climbed up and entered her bedroom. She didn't look back. No sense. She already heard Dusty driving to Marvin's house.

After she undressed, she put on her pajamas and lay down, pulling the covers over her.

She rested her hand on her breast.

Her body would never feel the same again.

How could it?

How could she?

Dusty Lincoln had happened to her.

She fell asleep smiling.

Before she knew it, it was time to get up. She rolled over and stretched, every cell in her body humming with energy and satisfaction.

She giggled and thought of taking out an ad in the paper to announce that she finally realized what all the hoopla was about.

After last night's amazing, satisfying encounter, she understood what everyone else had already known.

Sex was the best thing ever invented.

She'd come around to liking Dusty despite their rough start.

Even though she didn't respect charm for charm's sake, Dusty had enough awesome stuff going on underneath the charm. He wasn't a phony.

He'd given her a precious gift last night, the memories of which she would cherish for a lifetime.

She got up and jumped into the shower, only then noticing there was a spot of chocolate on her breast that Dusty had missed last night.

She'd never look at chocolate fondue the same way again. She'd never be able to drink a lime cooler, or lime anything, without thinking of Dusty. And sex.

Sensations washed through her.

Bits and pieces of memories flickered and warmed her.

Dear Lord, the man knew how to make love.

Laughing out loud, she washed herself and pronounced this day to be amazing.

Only one problem marred the beauty of last night's memories and today's energy.

Maxine Porter had fallen in love with Dustin Lincoln.

She hoped and prayed she could keep that from being problematic.

An hour later, she walked into the stable to find Dusty there ahead of her.

He looked as tired as she felt, but also as relaxed, a loosening up of bones and sinews and attitudes.

"Good morning," she said.

He glanced up from the horse he'd been brushing.

"Good morning to you, too!" He stepped around to the horse's far side so Max couldn't see his face. "Great day, eh?"

Where her tone had been quiet and satisfied, his was upbeat, but she frowned because it didn't ring true. Dusty used a fake hearty voice.

Aw, Dusty, she wanted to say, *you don't need to do fake this morning*. He'd given her a bout of fun. He'd taught her about lovemaking, and about how sex could take a woman to the stars and back again.

With her lack of experience in all things male and female, she didn't know what to do with her newfound love.

She didn't know how to act with Dusty, and how to be normal.

There was no more normal.

She might love the man, but she wasn't expecting forever. So why was he being so surface charmy?

Or was she just so gauche that she didn't know how to play the game?

Had last night been about his pity for her, or taking advantage of her?

Had she read all the signs wrong?

She didn't *know*.

Dusty was sophisticated.

She wasn't.

Maybe she should follow his lead and pretend she was cool with everything. But she wasn't. She was happy, downright bruised with radiance, while Dusty was his old happy-go-lucky self. It hurt…and she was so screwed up.

He'd given her one night. He hadn't promised a lifetime or an eternity, even though she was infinitely different and changed to her core.

She accepted that.

So what was he trying to tell her with his drastic mood swing from his middle-of-the-night tenderness to this morning's fakery?

She struggled to come up with ordinary talk.

"The revival committee is coming for tea this afternoon," she said quietly. "You'll finally have your chance to meet all of them."

"Heyyyy. Great. Looking forward to it."

Max stepped out of the stable and walked back to the house, to the office where she had bills to pay and a confused heart to nurse through to a realistic place.

They'd used condoms, so there would be no pregnancy.

He had given her a gift of sensuality and luminosity.

She could deal with it being a onetime thing. She could settle for less.

But, oh, she wanted more.

Chapter 11

When Max stepped out of the stable leaving Dusty alone, he leaned his head against Thunder's neck and exhaled sharply.

He hoped he'd been his normal carefree self with Max. He might have fooled her into thinking all was back to normal, but he didn't know for sure.

He wasn't an actor.

He wasn't used to subterfuge.

With Dusty, what you saw was what you got.

While she'd seemed happy to go back to normal, albeit a new quiet and relaxed normal, Dusty was rattled and confused.

Max had enjoyed every minute of last night. He'd made certain of that.

He'd enjoyed it, too. It had touched him more deeply than he had intended.

It was supposed to have been about her and only her. He was supposed to have been able to give her a gift and walk away unscathed. Untouched.

Dear Lordy, she'd touched him deep in his soul.

No. A great big no.

He hadn't intended that. It shouldn't be happening.

This morning she talked about the revival committee. She didn't seem to expect more. She hadn't hung all over him. She hadn't whispered sweet nothings about getting together the coming night.

She'd seemed content. Happy.

So why did he feel lost? Unmoored from reality? Unanchored in a sea of…of…

He didn't *know*.

He'd lost the harbor of his untroubled equilibrium.

Far as he could tell, she wasn't going to try to tie him down. She wasn't expecting more than what he had given her.

He smacked his hand against the stall railing, angry.

Angry?

He should be relieved that Max made no demands.

Why did it piss him off that she seemed satisfied and didn't want more?

She *should* ask for more. She deserved more.

She deserved some guy who would pamper her and move heaven and earth to make her happy.

She lived too serious an existence. Too many times in her life, she had settled for far less than she was worth.

Filled to the brim with outrage, he stomped toward the house and into the office.

"You deserve more fun, dammit."

She jumped up from her chair. It banged against the wall. "Dusty? Are you okay?"

"Did you hear what I said?"

"I think the entire county did."

"Well?"

"Well, what?" She spread her hands. "Dusty, I don't know what you want."

"Yeah, well, me, either. Okay?" And wasn't *that* the truth? And wasn't that the crux of his problems?

Unflappable, easygoing, devil-may-care Dustin Lincoln's calm existence had been shattered, blown out of the water by a lousy hamstring and a loose knee and a polo match and a woman who dressed like a man.

Everything had changed.

He wanted to go back to his first day here and to his not liking her. To not lov—

Oh, no. He did not almost think that.

No freaking way.

He yearned for his old, healthy, undamaged, carefree life.

He needed…needed… Aw, hell. He needed what?

"Dusty," Max said, "stop whatever is going on inside of your head. It was one night between a pair of consenting adults. You gave me a gift. I'm not expecting more. Okay?"

Okay. Yeah. Okay.

He stepped back out of the house onto the veranda. A twinge in his leg warned him to cut out the childish tantrum. All of Dusty's stomping around had hurt his knee.

He didn't like having a faulty leg.

He didn't like being damaged.

He liked to be whole and healthy and on top of the world.

Well, duh, Dusty, doesn't everyone?

His mom wouldn't believe him if she saw him in this state.

Dusty didn't stomp around.

She used to say that he didn't have a temper and that he'd never gone through the terrible twos.

She said he was the most even-tempered child she'd ever met.

Was she kidding herself, too proud of her offspring to recognize his faults?

Or was Dusty changing?

And if he was changing, why wasn't it for the better?

Why was he behaving worse?

Why did he *feel* worse?

Walking across the yard, the answer to his foul mood hit him like the ground coming up to meet him when a bull like Cyclone threw him off.

He wanted more of Max.

He wanted last night all over again.

And again and again and again.

Maxine Porter had burrowed in under his skin.

In early afternoon, Max raced back across the fields to the stable.

She'd scheduled the revival committee to come to her house as a chance for Dusty to meet everyone and to go over final plans before all of the participating rodeo riders arrived to practice in a couple of days.

Max had spent hours and hours on the phone these past few weeks organizing stable stalls and rooms and food and feed and on and on for the duration of their stay. The list had been endless.

Thank goodness she'd hired Dusty to take care of convincing all of these people to come.

Max rushed into the stable after helping to round up and fence in some cattle that had escaped. She did a fast job of currying Wind and then rushed across the yard.

All of her friends' cars were there, so everyone had already arrived.

By now, Marvin must have introduced Dusty to the members he hadn't yet met.

Plenty of chatter drifted out through the screen door.

Max toed off her boots and left them on the veranda.

Her stomach protested that she'd missed her lunch, but she could do nothing about it until after—

"Max doesn't have a clue, so everyone be careful that you don't tip her off." That was Vy's voice.

What did she mean about tipping Max off? To what?

"She would be furious," Nadine said. "I couldn't believe how hard it was the first time I saw you in the diner, Dusty, and had to pretend I didn't know why you were in town."

Bewildered, Max sucked in a quiet breath.

"Me, too," Vy said. "It was hard because I know how stubborn Max is. She would have been angry."

"Worse than that," Honey Armstrong piped up. "She would be hurt if she knew."

Hurt? An ominous dread settled into Max's empty stomach.

"I said right from the start this was a bad idea. I didn't like it then and I don't like it now. Someone has to tell her what you've done." That was Rachel, the mother of two who had married Travis Read after he came to town. So, one committee member hadn't agreed with the subterfuge. What subterfuge?

"I wish I'd never called you to come here, Dusty," Marvin said.

Marvin? What was he talking about? He hadn't called Dusty. Max had done the hiring herself.

A memory wound its way through her, of Marvin constantly singing Dustin Lincoln's praises and of him urging her to consider Dusty over the other candidates.

"For all the good it did," Marvin said. "I shouldn't have betrayed her."

And yet Marvin, the closest to a father figure Max had ever known, had betrayed her without a second thought. It was obvious he hadn't wanted any of her rodeo ideas to be implemented.

Otherwise, why bring in someone who'd been passionate about adding bull riding back in and, at the start at least, about getting rid of the polo?

Marvin hadn't acted alone. The entire committee had known why Dusty was here. Her girlfriends had betrayed her, too.

Her stomach cramped. She clutched her middle.

"Sure, we've still got the polo match to contend with," Dusty said, "but at least the bull riding is back on the agenda."

Like a haze lifting on a foggy day, everything cleared for Max.

Marvin had all but directed her to consider Dusty and no other. Why? Because the women who she had thought were friends had decided that her ideas lacked merit.

They had called this guy in to make her change her mind, not to help her to run the rodeo.

And yet, they had behaved as though they were surprised that she had hired someone. They had pretended to be indignant that she was spending the money.

Through every phase of her life she had known betrayal by the people she should have been able to trust.

Her father had died early in her life and her mother, the one person who should have protected her, had married a miserable, predatory man, only so that she wouldn't have to be alone.

Her mother should have had more courage. She and Max would have gotten by somehow.

Instead, she had exposed Max to *him*.

Then she had died, leaving Max in his care legally, with no option but to protect herself by her own wits.

Now the relationships she had forged with these women had also been proved to be false.

She saw Marvin in the corner watching her with dismay and guilt written all over his face.

Marvin. At one point he had been her savior. Now he was as guilty as the rest of them of treachery.

What was one more betrayal on top of all others?

It shouldn't hurt as much as it did.

She should be used to people not being who they said they were.

But it hurt. Oh, how she ached.

She wanted to curl up into a ball in a dark room and never face the light of day again.

Dusty! What had last night been about?

Had all of that sweetness been about changing her mind? About manipulating her?

He'd done a great job of it.

He turned around and saw her. His face fell. He reached out one hand to her.

"Max. I'm sorry. Don't—"

She didn't stay to hear what he had to say.

She raced upstairs to a chorus of women calling her name, but didn't throw herself onto the bed in a fit of self-pity.

When she heard other feet rushing up the stairs, she locked her door.

Someone pounded on it.

"Max, let's talk." Vy.

No. Let's not talk.

The time for talking had been months ago when they had decided to install a spy on her ranch.

In her *home.*

She gasped. Inside her body.

Instead of hiding under the covers, she hauled an old suitcase out of the back of her closet and threw in a handful of clothes and her few toiletries.

Hearing the urgency of a gaggle of women whispering outside her bedroom door, she couldn't go back out into the hallway, so she stalked to her window and opened it.

A grim smile formed on her lips. Dusty hadn't taken down the ladder.

After tossing her suitcase to the ground, she skimmed down the ladder, rushing to get away before anyone figured out what she was doing.

She couldn't stay here, not on this ranch with Marvin and Dusty, and not in this town with a committee full of women who hadn't had the least bit of faith in her.

At her truck, she tossed her suitcase into the bed.

Josh ran out from the stable. "Whatcha doin', Mom? Where are you going?"

"*We* are taking a small trip." She hadn't packed anything for him, but the ladies wouldn't have let her go down the hallway to Josh's room. They wouldn't have let her leave the house, or the ranch. Normally, she'd stand her ground— give a piece of her mind, if warranted. But these were her closest friends... She was so hurt and bewildered by it all she couldn't look any of them in the eye right now.

"Climb into the truck and put on your seat belt."

Josh followed orders, maybe intrigued by the spontaneity of it. Max never did anything on the spur of the moment.

They drove into town and Max stopped at the bank. She used the ATM to take her last four hundred dollars out of her lone account.

On the way back to the truck, she ran into Graham.

"Is Josh in the truck?" he asked.

Graham chose the wrong day to confront Max again. She'd had it with people hurting her. She poked her finger in Graham's chest.

"Listen to me, you snake. If you ever come near me again, or if you come near my son, I will tell everyone in this town about the things you tried to do to me when I was just a teenager."

"They wouldn't believe you."

"I sure would." The harsh female voice caught Max off guard and she spun around.

Eleanor Riddel, the owner of the local grocery store, lit a cigarette and exhaled roughly before saying, "I'd believe every word of it. Through the years, I've instructed the girls who work in my store to keep away from you."

About to step past Graham, she said, "The whole town

knows who you are, Graham. Leave Max and her son alone. She's a better person than you can ever hope to be."

Graham walked away heavily.

Max stared at Eleanor openmouthed. "I didn't realize anyone else knew."

"We didn't know things, but we sort of guessed. Remember how my hubby, God rest his soul, often came out to the ranch to hand-deliver your groceries?"

Max nodded.

"It was to check up on you. I told him to look for signs, you know, like bruising."

Max remembered other people coming out. How the mechanic would insist that he could deliver Graham's car when it was done. He would also insist on saying hi to Max.

She remembered the way he used to look at her, and now she knew why. He was checking for signs of damage.

The people in town had been monitoring the situation, all while she had thought she was alone.

"If he comes around you again," Eleanor said, "I'll head out to his ranch and kick him in the nuts myself."

Max smiled. Somehow, she had the feeling Graham was history in her life.

"Thank you, Eleanor, but I think he got the message."

Max climbed back into her truck, warmed by the invisible support that had always been here for her, but still reeling from the betrayal that the people closest to her should have never committed.

She drove on out of town toward… She didn't know. She didn't have a clue where to go.

If she and Josh stayed in hotels or motels, her money would last only a few days.

She had no one on whom to depend.

She was lost.

Only one person had been really and truly kind to her lately, and irony of ironies, it had been Dusty's mother.

Taking a chance and pulling onto the shoulder of the road, she retrieved her cell phone from her pocket and punched in the number Dusty had given her.

When Charlie answered, Max said only, "Where do you live?"

There must have been distress in her voice, because Charlie gave her directions and then asked, "Are you coming now?"

"Yeah," Max whispered.

"Good. See you soon, sweetie."

Max ended the connection and pulled back onto the highway.

An uncertain voice from the passenger seat said, "Mom?" Josh sounded small and insecure. Guilt flooded Max.

"We're taking a holiday, just you and me," she said, voice as fake hearty as Dusty's had been this morning. She winced. "That'll be fun, won't it, buddy?"

Buddy. She'd never used that term with her son before. She was the adult and he was the kid.

They weren't buddies.

They were mother and child, and she loved him more than she loved anyone or anything else on this earth.

Dragging him away from home might not be smart, but she would have never left him behind.

By the time she turned onto Charlie's property, Josh was sound asleep, head lolling and drool running from the side of his mouth.

Charlie, seated on a big wicker armchair on a broad flat veranda, stood and crossed the yard.

Max got out of the truck and walked into her arms.

She stayed there, both on Charlie's ranch and in Charlie's loving, supportive presence, for two whole weeks.

* * *

Dusty had taken one look at Max's stricken face and realized how badly he'd screwed up.

Before he had ever had sex with her, he should have told her the truth of why he'd come to Rodeo.

Truth to tell, he'd forgotten. He'd become so involved in the rodeo and so invested in its success that the whys and wherefores of having arrived here had no longer mattered.

He should have known how much it would matter to Max.

Last night, he'd learned that under her testiness and bad humor was a heart of pure generous gold.

She loved with passion. In her inexperienced zeal, she gave as good as she got.

If she were to ever give over completely to passion 100 percent, if she were to ever fall in love, that man would be one hell of a lucky guy.

Once Maxine Porter started loving she would never stop.

She had her head screwed on right.

Last night, he'd thought it a onetime affair. He'd thought he was doing it for her, but no. From the start, even while she'd confounded him, he'd wanted her.

Last night had been for him as much as for her.

It had been a beginning.

In blissful ignorance, he had missed how right it was.

It *should* have been the beginning of more and more happiness to come.

But he'd screwed up.

He hadn't realized the pure, perfect bliss of spending time with Max, and that one night would never be enough.

He'd given her a night of loving and she had given him awareness, a crack in his carefree shell to a depth of feeling he'd never known before and a burgeoning love that he had just killed because he'd been careless.

He'd dealt with her heart with a cavalier disregard for all that he had been giving, but also taking.

He hadn't *known*.

Now Dusty would never be part of a loving future they should have been starting with last night's brilliant love-making.

Not sex. *Love*making.

He'd never experienced lovemaking before.

It had been life-changing.

After the first week, Dusty gave up trying to find Max and Josh, as did Marvin and the revival committee.

He worked tirelessly on the rodeo, driven by a need to prove, for Max's sake, that she had been right all along.

He worked to prove not only himself wrong, but also Marvin, the ladies and everyone in town.

Too late, only after the cowboys and all the city boys had arrived and started practicing and people started to get excited about the whole unlikely venture, did Dusty realize that Max had really been onto something big.

A polo match in a Western rodeo was about as unique as unique could be.

Buzz about it popped up all over the place. It intrigued the public. Nadine interviewed both the rodeo riders and the polo players.

Local TV programs interviewed Dusty.

The ladies thought his good looks and charm made him the perfect spokesperson, but he agreed to the interviews only so he could sing Maxine Porter's praises.

He could have found no bigger way to screw up with her than to betray her, and left himself with no possibility of salvation. But he had to try.

Their one night together haunted him and kept him awake at night.

For the first time in his life, he craved another night with her—more moonlight, starlight, chocolate, lime coolers and fun. More pickup truck sex. More loving of Max's body and spirit.

More getting to know her.

He filled his days with practice for the rodeo and the polo match, but also with running Max's ranch.

At night he fell into bed exhausted, but inconsolable. He ached for Max. He lay awake staring at the ceiling.

He wanted her to come home to a viable business and successful rodeo.

Aw, hell, he just wanted her to come home.

Charlie took Max shopping.

Max hated shopping, especially for clothes.

"I don't have any money," she said. Her four hundred dollars had to last until she could find a job. Then she had to find a place for them to live and a sitter for Josh since school was still out.

At the moment, her son was out on the range, up in the saddle in front of Dusty's father. They'd taken to each other like horses to hay.

Max chewed on her thumbnail.

For the hundredth time, Charlie gently pulled her hand away from her mouth.

"We're going shopping and you are going to enjoy it," Charlie said, tone implacable. "Dusty's father and I will cover the costs."

"Oh, but you can't."

"Oh, but I can and I will."

In the week since Max had arrived, she had learned how useless it was arguing with Charlene. Charlie got what she wanted, mainly because she read Max better than anyone ever had.

She tapped into Max's secret longings.

Now that Max had spare time on her hands without the constant, grinding stress of running the ranch and worrying about finances, she recognized all that she had missed over the years. Even after she realized the fair had already started at home in Rodeo, she barely gave it a second thought.

Dusty had given her a taste of adolescence.

Charlie was giving her a taste of female adulthood spent with a friend.

They drove to the nearest town with a spa for a day of pampering.

They bought Max new clothes, still the jeans and shirts that she favored, yeah, but prettier than the stuff she usually wore for mucking out stables.

She got her hair cut while Charlie hovered giving instructions.

The hairstylist streamlined what had been a hack job on Max's part, and suddenly Max had big eyes and high cheekbones.

They both got manicures.

Max balked.

Charlie insisted.

Charlie won.

Max enjoyed.

They drank margaritas with lunch, and Charlie limited Max to only two. Max loved that she cared enough to set limits.

She loved that Charlie treated her like a daughter.

Charlie cared for her.

Charlie kept her safe.

Max sat in the passenger seat of Charlie's little car on the drive back to the ranch, a mild contented buzz mellowing her into happiness.

Or as much happiness as she could feel given that she

wasn't on her own ranch, in her own home, sleeping in her own bed.

Charlie's house might be beautiful and the people warm and friendly, but everywhere Max turned she saw photographs of Dusty and heard stories of his childhood and his rodeo career.

That night, wrapped in a plush bathrobe sitting in front of a roaring fire in the Lincolns' big family room, Charlie answered her phone.

Max shamelessly eavesdropped on the private conversation, wrapped in a plush bathrobe of her own. She admired her pink toenails.

For a long time, Charlie just listened before starting to intersperse comments.

"No…Yes. I know you're sad and don't know what to do. I know you miss her…That much, huh?…Yes, I do feel bad for you, honey. I wish I could help you, but I can't."

After Charlie disconnected, Max asked, "Dusty?"

Charlie nodded. "He's missing you. Are you sure you don't want him to know you're here? Are you sure you don't want to talk to him?"

Max shook her head. "No. Don't tell him."

Charlie turned to her husband and said, "Would you mind leaving us alone for a while?"

Big, masculine, handsome Angus said, "Sure thing, honey," and left the room.

Of Max, she asked, "Are you ready to tell me what happened with my son?"

"Oh, Charlie," Max, embarrassed and chagrined and humiliated, said, "I've been as dumb as every other woman in the state."

"How so?"

"I fell in love with your son."

Charlie sat back with a smile on her lips. "Well, of

course, you did. But you're not talking about infatuation like all of those other women, are you? You're talking about a deep love."

Max nodded.

"You might as well tell me all about it," Charlie said.

And Max did.

Half an hour later, Charlie said, "You do know it isn't one-sided, right?"

Max stared at her, afraid to believe what she implied.

"He's in love with you, too," Charlie continued. "I've never heard Dusty so upset about a woman. He's worried about you to the depths of his soul. He's frightened that you're all alone somewhere without support."

Max lifted a finger to her lips to bite her nail, but caught sight of the pretty pink enamel on the nail and lowered her hand to her lap. "Do you think I should talk to him? Should I tell him how much I love him?"

"Hell, no," Charlie said with a deep laugh. "Let him stew awhile longer."

So Max did.

Cradled in the oasis of the Lincoln ranch, she rested for the first time in two decades, and grew into a strong sense of herself and her value.

In the days leading up to the opening of the fair and rodeo, Dusty struggled to be his normal self.

Dusty had given away a piece of himself to Max and he wanted it back.

That piece of nonsense didn't rate a second thought, especially since he didn't understand what he meant.

Throughout the arrival of the rodeo riders and their horses, through the many exhausting and exhilarating polo practices on the field preparing for the match at the back of the fairgrounds, he tried to stay focused on the job he'd come here to do. And despite the fun of watching city slickers try to learn Western events, and cowboys and cowgirls learning polo—all through the exciting hubbub of the first week and a half of the fair—Dusty struggled to hold it all together.

Day after day for two weeks, he worked from six in the morning until midnight, and he did it all for Max.

He'd taken her trust and had betrayed it.

He had also taken any bit of enjoyment she might have received from the success of the rodeo.

This had been her baby, not his.

He did the work now, only because he couldn't find her, but he planned to give her all of the credit.

Up until the night before the polo match, he fooled himself into thinking that he could walk away from this town—and from Max—scot-free. He thought that once the fair and rodeo were done, he could leave here and be the same carefree footloose man he had always been.

Lying awake the night before the match, he no longer hid from the truth.

He missed Max with an ache that left him breathless.

He'd fallen in love with her.

Chapter 12

Dusty stepped out onto Marvin's porch early on Saturday morning and breathed deeply of fresh clear air.

A good day had dawned for a polo match. A *great* day.

If only Max were here, it would be more than great. It would be perfect.

He loaded up most of the items he would need for the day.

Marvin had driven the ponies and horses over already.

Dusty had just picked up the last saddle to load into the back of his truck when he heard someone enter the stable.

He stepped into the aisle and stopped cold.

Max.

She stood silhouetted against the sunlight streaming into the yard. She seemed slimmer.

Changes in her registered right away. The clothes she wore actually fit her. They weren't much different from her old clothes, except that they were new, and they fit. And she had a pretty body.

But he knew that already.

He knew her body.

He knew her.

He understood her now.

Dropping the saddle, he stalked the length of the aisle, not stopping until he hauled her into his arms and kissed the daylights out of her.

She didn't respond.

He didn't stop.

In slow degrees, his lips urged hers to open beneath the tender onslaught of his mouth.

She gave in and he lifted her into his arms, against his

chest, trying to take her inside of him to carry in his heart forever.

When he came up for air, he slid her down his body and cradled her face between his hands. "Don't leave again."

She stared with wide, searching eyes. He hoped she could see how much he loved her.

"Don't *ever* leave me again," he repeated.

She nodded, but whispered, "We need to talk."

"Later."

He kissed her again until a gaggle of women's voices interrupted.

"Max! Vy saw you drive through town. We piled into her car and got here as fast as we could."

"My God, Max. You're home."

"Forgive us. We love you."

"We're so sorry."

Dusty lifted his head and ordered, "Leave."

He kissed Max again, but those pesky women's voices wouldn't stop.

"Leave," he roared and there was silence.

To the women, Max said, "We'll talk later," and picked up where he'd left off kissing her.

He heard whispering and shushing and receding footsteps and a car engine driving out of the laneway. They had the stable to themselves. It was his and hers. Theirs.

Taking Max's hand, he pulled her to the stairs to the hayloft and urged her up with a hand on her bottom.

He followed her up.

Once there, he made love to her, undressing her as though she were a rare treasure.

She undressed him, too, with wonder in her eyes that he knew was reflected in his own gaze on her.

He was never letting her go again.

Afterward, they lay sated in each other's arms and Dusty had found his home.

"I can't lose you again," Dusty said while he feathered fingers down her spine. "I love you."

"I know."

He rose up onto one elbow and looked down at her. "Yeah? How?"

"Your mom told me."

Dusty laughed. "She knows me well. She's right."

They started to make love a second time, but then Dusty jumped up to raid Josh's stash of potato chips.

"I want to make love and you want to eat chips?" Max sounded so put out that Dusty laughed.

"It's the way I want to eat them that you'll like." He opened a bag of barbecue chips and crushed a handful of them over her breasts.

Moments later, he had licked and tickled and kissed and eaten so many chips off Max's body she squirmed with delight.

Both of their cell phones intruded, over and over, with people calling to get them to the fair, no doubt.

Dusty sighed and sat up. He swiped salt from his chin.

"We'd better go," he said, "but we're finishing this tonight."

They dressed.

"I like that lacy pink bra," Dusty said. "Sure beats the old athletic sport ones."

He had trouble taking his eyes off Max. He'd almost lost her and couldn't believe she'd come back. To him. Not to the rodeo, but here to the ranch, to him.

They drove to the fair in Dusty's truck and parked with the other competitors' vehicles.

Grabbing Max's hand, Dusty rushed to the grounds

on which the polo match would take place. A huge crowd waited. The stands were packed.

Dusty turned to Max with a grin. "You were right. They're here on curiosity alone, but wait until they watch the match. It'll thrill them."

He kissed her. "You made this possible."

Max frowned and scratched her chest. She reached inside her shirt and pulled something out of her bra. A potato chip.

Dusty laughed and took it from her. He popped it into his mouth then leaned forward and kissed Max. When he pulled back, her eyes were wide and the chip was in her mouth.

She chewed, swallowed and laughed. "Oh, Dusty, I do love you."

"Max, I got so many tricks to show you it'll take a lifetime to go through them all."

"Dusty?"

"Yeah?"

"I have a lifetime to give."

He stilled. "Seriously? 'Cause I do, too."

Someone called Dusty's name and she sounded anxious and angry.

Vy came running. "Get to your team right now. Sam is having a fit waiting. Everyone's waiting. It's time for the match to start."

Dusty grinned at Max and said, "Wish me luck."

He ran to the ponies. A minute later, he mounted up with a heart more full than it had ever been, shouted, "Yeehaw!" and the match officially started.

Vy enveloped Max in a hug.

"I'm so sorry, Max," she whispered, voice husky and emotional. "We're sorry. All of us. Betraying you is the worst thing I've ever done in my life."

With reserves of anger that still bothered her, Max tried

to resist Vy, but couldn't. This was her good friend. And Vy realized her mistake and how huge it had been.

Max pulled back and said, "It's okay. We'll get past this."

Vy's violet eyes filled with hope. "Promise?"

"I promise. Friendship is always worth working on."

"Good. I don't want to ever lose your friendship again."

A cheer went up from the crowd.

"Come on," Max said, filled with joy. "I don't want to miss the game."

Hand in hand, Max and Vy ran to the special spot cordoned off for the organizers and watched one of the most fun, farcical and exciting events that had ever happened on the Rodeo Fairgrounds.

It captivated and entertained and did everything Max had hoped it would.

At the end of the match, the crowd wandered away happy and buzzing.

Max heard more than one person say things along the lines of "I didn't think I'd like that, but now I'm hoping they'll do it again next year."

The woman's friend replied, "Maybe next year the cowboys will win."

The first woman said, "The city boys didn't do too well in the barrel racing yesterday."

The second lady said, "It sure was fun to watch," and they walked away laughing.

Vy smiled at Max. "You were right."

"Yeah," Max said. "Vindication is sweet."

Dusty ran out of the arena area and gave Max a great big hug.

"That was amazing." He lifted her off her feet and swung her around. "You were right all along."

The revival committee crowded around.

Dusty looked at every one of them and said, "We were all wrong. Thank God you didn't give up."

Max said, "I'm glad I didn't give in to pressure to quit."

Charlie and Angus Lincoln approached, each holding one of Josh's hands.

"That was fun, Dusty." Josh's little pipsqueak voice cut through the noise of the crowd. "I want to do that someday."

Dusty stared at his parents holding Josh's hands. "They were with you?"

Charlie nodded and stepped close to him.

"I'm glad they were safe," Dusty said, "but shouldn't your loyalty be to me?"

Charlie kissed his cheek. "Someone else needed me for a while."

Dusty smiled. "Thanks for taking care of my girl."

Before Max could object that she was capable of taking care of herself, Marvin approached.

Max didn't know what to do about Marvin. Once upon a time, he had saved her and her son from destitution.

Then he had betrayed her.

What was she to think?

"Could I have a word with you?" he asked.

She stepped away from the group, but sensed the intensity of their regard.

One thing she knew about the inhabitants of Rodeo was that they cared about each other.

Marvin scuffed the toe of one of his boots in the dirt. "I've never done anything worse in my life." He refused to look at her, but hung his head and ran a finger under his nose.

"You're like a daughter to me," he mumbled. "You and Josh are the only family I have. I should have trusted you."

He looked at her then, with all of his misery etched on his tanned and wrinkled face. "I'm sorry, Max."

Her pulse pounded so hard in her ears, she barely heard his rough, quiet apology.

Max wrapped her arms around Marvin. When all was said and done, he was the only father figure she had. And she loved him.

It wouldn't be smart to throw him away.

While true that he should have had more faith in her, as should all of her friends, she had enough understanding that her ideas had been pretty far off the wall for them to envision the way she had.

She heard Marvin sniff. When she let him go, he turned away, pulled a large handkerchief out of his pocket and blew his nose.

"You're a better person than me, Max," he said, "and I thank you for your forgiveness."

Before she had a chance to tell him she loved him, he walked away, probably because the emotions had become too intense.

"Mom, can we go to the petting zoo? I want to see the baby animals."

Max cleared heavy emotions from her throat and said, "Sure, Josh, but first we have to watch Dusty's bull riding."

"No," Dusty said.

Max held up her hand, understanding why Dusty wouldn't want her there. Maybe her nerves would transfer to him. "Dusty, it's hard for me to watch, but if you're going to be in it, I'm going to watch. I'll be fine. That's final."

Dusty took her arm in his and drew her away from the group. She noticed his limp and frowned.

"Why are you still limping after so long?" she asked.

"All of the practicing for the polo match took its toll." He leaned close. "Max, I didn't enter the bull riding."

She stopped walking. "You didn't enter? After persuading me to have it? Why not?"

"I was afraid I would injure my knee permanently. I could do only one discipline in the rodeo."

"Then why participate in the polo match? Why not just bull ride?"

"I wanted to honor you. After all of your trouble getting the polo included, how could I turn my back on it?"

"You mean you chose the polo match over bull riding for me?"

He stopped and looked down at her with all of the love that seemed to be in his heart, and all of it aimed at her.

Max's own heart almost burst with happiness, with a quiet joy that she hadn't known since the birth of her son.

That had been the most special event of her life, but the joy had been tempered by fear of not knowing how to take care of this new little creature on her own?

But this? With Dusty? Pure, unadulterated jubilation. Nothing prevented her from giving herself over to it completely.

"I don't need bull riding," Dusty said.

"At all?"

"I'm high on life, Max. I'm high on love for you. I don't need eight seconds of terror to affirm that I'm alive."

"No more bull riding?"

"No more bull riding."

"You would give it up for me? Not just for today, but for always?"

"Yeah, I would. Same with all the rodeo events. If you'll have me as a partner, I want to help you run the ranch."

"Really?"

"Yeah, really. You've been doing an amazing job, but you need help and I need to be close to you. These past couple weeks, I've enjoyed working on the ranch as much as setting up this rodeo."

He brushed his hand across her new, refined haircut.

"What do you think, Maxine Porter? Are you up for a partner in ranching and parenthood and life? For a partner in love?"

Max's heart split open with bliss.

"Yeah, Dusty Lincoln. I'm up for all of that."

She rested her head on his shoulder. "There's one thing I won't abide in my house, though, Dusty."

"What's that? Wet towels on the bathroom floor?"

"No."

"Whiskers in the sink?"

"Nope."

"Empty toilet paper rolls?"

"Not even that."

"Then what?"

Max giggled. "No cowboy of mine is ever, ever allowed to wear macramé around his neck."

Dusty threw back his head and shouted with laughter.

* * * * *

*"Brenda Harlen writes couples with such great
chemistry and characters to root for."*
—New York Times *bestselling author Linda Lael Miller*

*The story of committed bachelor Liam Gilmore,
rancher turned innkeeper, and his brand-new manager,
Macy Clayton. She's clearly off-limits, but Liam can't
resist being pulled into her family of adorable triplets!
Is Liam suddenly dreaming of forever after with the
single mom?*

*Read on for a sneak preview of
the next great book in the Match Made in Haven
miniseries,* Claiming the Cowboy's Heart
by Brenda Harlen.

"You kissed me," he reminded her.

"The first time," she acknowledged.

"You kissed me back the second time."

"Has any woman ever not kissed you back?" she
wondered.

"I'm not interested in any other woman right now," he
told her. "I'm only interested in you."

The intensity of his gaze made her belly flutter. "I've
got three kids," she reminded him.

"That's not what's been holding me back."

"What's holding you back?"

"I'm trying to respect our working relationship."

"Yeah, that complicates things," she agreed. Then she finished the wine in her glass and pushed away from the table. "Will you excuse me for a minute? I just want to give my mom a call to check on the kids."

"Of course," he agreed. "But I can't promise the rest of that tart will be there when you get back."

She gave one last, lingering glance at the pastry before she said, "You can finish the tart."

He was tempted by the dessert, but he managed to resist. He didn't know how much longer he could hold out against his attraction to Macy—or if she wanted him to.

Had he crossed a line by flirting with her? She hadn't reacted in a way that suggested she was upset or offended, but she hadn't exactly flirted back, either.

"Is everything okay?" he asked when she returned to the table several minutes later.

She nodded. "I got caught in the middle of an argument."

"With your mom?"

"With myself."

His brows lifted. "Did you win?"

"I hope so," she said.

Then she set an antique key on the table and slid it toward him.

Don't miss
Claiming the Cowboy's Heart *by Brenda Harlen,*
available February 2019 wherever
Harlequin® *Special Edition books and ebooks are sold.*

www.Harlequin.com

Looking for more satisfying love stories
with community and family at their core?

Check out **Harlequin® Special Edition**
and **Love Inspired®** books!

New books available every month!

CONNECT WITH US AT:

Facebook.com/groups/HarlequinConnection

Facebook.com/HarlequinBooks

Twitter.com/HarlequinBooks

Instagram.com/HarlequinBooks

Pinterest.com/HarlequinBooks

ReaderService.com

HARLEQUIN®

**ROMANCE WHEN
YOU NEED IT**

HFGENRE2018

Earn points on your purchase of new Harlequin books from participating retailers.

Turn your points into **FREE BOOKS** of your choice!

Join for FREE today at **www.HarlequinMyRewards.com.**

Harlequin My Rewards is a free program (no fees) without any commitments or obligations.

MYR18